Ernest De Lancey Pierson

The Merry Muse

Society verse by American writers

Ernest De Lancey Pierson

The Merry Muse
Society verse by American writers

ISBN/EAN: 9783337386337

Printed in Europe, USA, Canada, Australia, Japan

Cover: Foto ©Andreas Hilbeck / pixelio.de

More available books at **www.hansebooks.com**

THE MERRY MUSE

SOCIETY VERSE

BY AMERICAN WRITERS

EDITED BY

ERNEST DE LANCEY PIERSON

Editor of "Society Verse"; Author of "Shadow of the Bars,"
"A Slave of Circumstances," etc.

———

NEW AND ENLARGED EDITION

———

CHICAGO, NEW YORK, AND SAN FRANCISCO
BELFORD, CLARKE & CO.
PUBLISHERS
LONDON: H. J. DRANE, LOVELL'S COURT, PATERNOSTER ROW

TO

Mrs. JAMES BARROW

("AUNT FANNY")

PREFATORY NOTE.

The friendly reception of "Society Verse, by American Writers," has encouraged the editor to prepare this larger and more representative collection, now published under the title of "The Merry Muse."

In a country where Pan is fast becoming a household divinity, it has been found impossible to collect in one volume specimens by all the scholars in this merry school of song. A sufficient selection has been made to display whatever variety of style and subject is to be found in the best vers de société by American Writers.

The rules that govern what is called the "Patrician Poetry" of the Old World cannot properly be applied to these lively lyrics of the New. And yet what our average verse lacks in polish and dignity of expression is more than atoned for by the spirit of native humor that pervades nearly every line.

It has been thought best not to hold any reserved seats in this symposium of singers.

Here brown heads and gray are grouped democratically, and it is to be hoped amicably, together. May their pleasant pipings stir a responsive and sympathetic chord in the public's feelings and finances, is the sincere wish of the subscriber.

ERNEST DE LANCEY PIERSON.

New York, January 12.

ACKNOWLEDGMENTS.

The editor would acknowledge the courtesy of the following publishers in allowing the use of valuable copyrights:—To Messrs Charles Scribner's Sons, selections from "Airs from Arcady," by H. C. Bunner ; Cassell & Company, selections from "Oberon and Puck," by Helen Gray Cone, and "Pipes from Prairie Land," by Minnie Gilmore ; D. Lothrop & Co., selections from "With Reed & Lyre," by Clinton Scollard, and "Post-Laureate Idyls," by Oscar Fay Adams ; Ticknor & Co., for selections from "Vagrant Verse," by Charles Henry Webb, and "Songs and Satires," by J. J. Roche ; Roberts and Brothers, for "Provençal Lovers," by E. C. Stedman, from "The Masque of the Poets"; Henry Holt & Co., selections from "A Midsummer Lark," by W. A. Crofut ; Keppler & Schwarzmann, for verses by C. C. Starkweather, Madeline Bridges, R. K. Munkittrick, Gertrude Hall, and A. E. Watrous ; Houghton, Mifflin & Co., for selections from the works of John G. Saxe, Oliver Wendell Holmes, Bret Harte, and Edmund Clarence Stedman ; Harper and Brothers, for "De Convenance," by Mrs. M. P. Handy, "A Kiss," by Joel Benton and "One of the Pack," by George Parsons Lathrop, in the "Monthly Magazine" ; "The Judge" Publishing Company, for verses by DeWitt Sterry ; Porter and Coates, for selections from "Mask and Domino," by David L. Proudfit ; Cupples, Hurd & Co., for selections from "Songs at the Start," Louise Guiney ; The Cosmopolitan Magazine Company, for verses by Duffield Osborne and Edith Tupper ; and The Century Company for the following poems from "The Century" Magazine : "Marjorie's Kisses," "Time's Revenge." and "On the Fly-Leaf of a Book of Old Plays." by Walter Learned : "To Mrs Carlyle," and "The Message of the Rose," by Bessie Chandler ; "Her Bonnet," by Mary Wilkins ; "The Fair Copyholder," by Charles Crandall ; "Le Grenier," by Robertson Trowbridge ; "In Winter," by Louise Chandler Moulton ; "The Morning After," by Harold Van Santvoord ; "Last July," by Sophy Lawrence ; "In Arcadia," by R. T. W. Duke ; "Two Triolets," by Harrison Robertson ; "Rondeaux of Cities," by Robert Grant ; "On a Hymn Book," by W. J. Henderson ; and "The Critic" Company, for verses by Irving Brown.

CONTENTS.

CONTENTS

WHERE ARE THE PIPES OF PAN?

OSCAR FAY ADAMS.

IN these prosaic days
  Of politics and trade,
When seldom Fancy lays
  Her touch on man or maid,
The sounds are fled that strayed
Along sweet streams that ran;
  Of song the world's afraid:
Where are the Pipes of Pan?

Within the busy maze
  Wherein our feet are stayed,
There roam no gleesome fays
  Like those which once repaid
  His sight who first essayed
The stream of song to span;
  Those spirits all are laid:
Where are the Pipes of Pan?

Dry now the poet's bays;
  Of song-robes disarrayed
He hears not now the praise
  Which erst those won who played
  On pipes of rushes made,
Before dull days began
  And love of song decayed:
Where are the Pipes of Pan?

ENVOY.

Prince, all our pleasures fade;
  Vain all the toils of man;
And Fancy cries dismayed,
  " Where are the Pipes of Pan? "

ON AN INTAGLIO HEAD OF MINERVA.

THOMAS BAILEY ALDRICH.

B ENEATH the warrior's helm, behold
The flowing tresses of the woman!
Minerva, Pallas, what you will —
A winsome creature, Greek or Roman.

Minerva? No! 'tis some sly minx
In cousin's helmet masquerading;
If not — then Wisdom was a dame
For sonnets and for serenading!

I thought the goddess cold, austere,
Not made for love's despairs and blisses,
Did Pallas wear her hair like that?
Was Wisdom's mouth so shaped for kisses?

The Nightingale should be her bird,
And not the Owl, big-eyed and solemn;
How very fresh she looks, and yet
She's older far than Trajan's Column!

3

The magic hand that carved this face,
   And set this vine-work round it running,
Perhaps ere mighty Phidias wrought
   Had lost its subtle skill and cunning.

Who was he ? Was he glad or sad,
   Who knew to carve in such a fashion ?
Perchance he graved the dainty head
   For some brown girl that scorned his passion.

Perchance, in some still garden place
   Where neither fount nor tree to-day is,
He flung the jewel at the feet
   Of Phryne, or perhaps 'twas Laïs.

But he is dust; we may not know
   His happy or unhappy story :
Nameless, and dead these centuries
   His work outlives him — there's his glory !

Both man and jewel lay in earth
   Beneath a lava-buried city :
The countless summers came and went
   With neither haste nor hate nor pity.

Years blotted out the man, but left
   The jewel fresh as any blossom,
Till some Visconti dug it up —
   To rise and fall on Mabel's bosom.

O nameless brother! See how Time
Your gracious handiwork has guarded;
See how your loving, patient art
Has come at last to be rewarded.

Who would not suffer slights of men,
And pangs of hopeless passion also,
To have his carven agate stone
On such a bosom rise and fall so!

DURANT LE DINER.

HENRY W. AUSTIN.

YOU in the sunshine, I in the shadow—
   Thus we have journeyed our whole life long
You in the calm of your Eldorado—
   I in my tempest of song.

Fortune held us in equal favor
   When we started with youthful hearts ;
Then she jilted me.   I forgave her,
   For she left me the lovely Arts.

Ah ! she could not of them bereave me ,
   They were mine from my first full breath
And their splendors will never leave me
   Till the sunset that men call death.

Strange, in sooth, is the retrospection !
   Strange the manifold parts I played
Chasing ever Delight's reflection,
   Half enamored of Sorrow's shade !

You and I—what a contrast, truly !
  I with passionate, purple veins :
You alone in the Ultima Thule
  Of Frigidity's sordid gains.

You a mountainous marvel of money,
  With your juleps that told of mints :
I a vagabond, strange and funny,
  Called Bohemia's facile Prince.

Miser, yours was a shoddy Palace ;
  Venus and Bacchus held court in mine ;
Deeper, I swear, have I drunk Life's chalice
  And even the dregs to my taste are fine.

All my tears I have turned to laughter—
  Melted like pearls in a nectar bowl.
What though nothing may be hereafter,
  Here, at least, I have had my soul.

Yes, I have had it and found it splendid—
  Psyche, Butterfly, Dream Divine !
What ! So soon must it all be ended ?
  Double the perfumes and spice the wine.

"Sorrow comes in the guise of pleasure ? "
  Trite, I'm certain, but may be true ;
Therefore bring me a broader measure,
  Bring me a weed of a darker hue.

You may sneer, you ill-savored sinner :
　　Wealth and power were denied my wits ;
Still I'm sure (when I've had my dinner)
　　That my misses outmatch your hits.

But what odds, when the play is over,
　　If men fancy you've won the game,
Since, though always you lived in clover
　　We beneath it will sleep the same ?

LOVE IS A KNAVE.

ARLO BATES.

L OVE is a knave ; he plucks a rose
Or twines a curl, and toys like this
He spreads to snare fond hearts ; he knows
How little else than light breath goes
To vows and bubbles both, I wis.

The most bewitching airs he blows
On sweet-voiced pipes ; while promised bliss,
Pledged with no sure fruition, shows
Love is a knave.

Sweet, to deprive us of repose,
Love weaves his schemes ; but naught amiss,
We laugh to scorn his threatened woes,
And cry, with warmest clasp and kiss,
Love is a knave !

9

TRIOLET.

ARLO BATES.

WEE Rose is but three,
    Yet coquettes she already.
I can scarcely agree
Wee Rose is but three,
When her archness I see!
    Are the sex born unsteady ?—
Wee Rose is but three,
    Yet coquettes she already.

A KISS—BY MISTAKE.

JOEL BENTON.

UPON the railway train we met—
  She had the softest, bluest eyes.
A face you never could forget—
  "Sixteen" with all that that implies.
I knew her once a little girl,
  And meeting now a mutual friend,
Our thoughts and hearts got in a whirl ;
  We talked for miles without much end.

I threw my arm around the seat
  Where, just in front, she sideways sat,
Her melting eyes and face to meet—
  (And no one wondered much at that)
For soon the station where she left
  Would on the sorrowing vision rise,
And I at least should feel bereft ;
  I thought a tear stood in her eyes.

She was but kith, not kin of mine ;
  Ten years had passed since last we met,
And when in going she did incline
  Her face, 'twas natural to forget,

It seemed so like a child I knew—
    I met her half way by mistake ,
And coming near those eyes of blue,
    She gently kissed me—*by mistake !*

She saw her error, and straightway ran
    With flaming blushes, rosy red ;
I should not be one-half a man
    If thoughts of wrong came in my head ;
In fact, I'd take that very train
    And travel daily for her sake,
If she would only come again
    And gently kiss me—*by mistake !*

CALLED BACK.

ALBERT ELLERY BERG.

THERE'S a lull in this dull Lenten season
  Of dressing and dancing, et cet. —
My thoughts turn from folly and treason,
  To one whom I cannot forget ;
Your last note is now almost yellow ;
  We quarreled — the usual way ;
I smiled upon some other fellow,
  Because you were flirting with May.

And when we went home from the party,
  Your looks were as cold as the air ;
I, too, was reserved, and no hearty
  Good-night kiss was asked for Mon Cher !
The next day I wrote you a letter
  Affecting a dignified tone,
And told you I thought it were better
  In future to leave me alone.

My pride led me then to deceive you,
  To tell you my love was all dead,
So foolish was I to believe you
  Would read 'twixt the lines — but instead—

You thought me in earnest, and parted,
  To worship society's calf;
But, Jack, I am now broken-hearted,
  And you are too tender by half.

We have been far too much to each other,
  To sever for nothing at all,
And if you have not found another,
  Why, then — you are welcome to call.
There's always a seat at our table,
  A place for you still in my heart;
So, Jack, if you think you are able,
  Come back and rehearse your old part!

A CANDID PROPOSAL.

JOHN PAUL BOCOCK.

I LOVE you, love you ! love you !! — yet confess
 A consciousness of trifling does come o'er me
When all the other shapes of loveliness
 To whom I've said the same thing rise before me.
They were, you are, the idol of my heart ;
 An idol it must have — which must be kissed. Hence
That which was once but of my life a part
 Is now my whole existence.

I see a scornful light grow in your. eyes,
 And yet they shine like stars half hid by mists
Magnificent ! You are the fairest prize
 My errant heart e'er fought for in love's lists.
You see, I'm candid ; you have bowled me over,
 And now I drink and dine and bathe in love ;
I puzzled half an hour just to discover
 The perfume of your glove !

But now all empty was this heart of mine ;
 Some woman must be in it. With that rose
Give me yourself, and walk into the shrine
 Its sovereign goddess. In short, I propose —
My ! Won't the Johnson-Mowbrays be enraged !
 This summer's changed the lot of many a rover —
That you and I be genuinely engaged
 Until the season's over !

2*   15

TO A FRIEND ON HIS WEDDING DAY.

JOHN PAUL BOCOCK.

SO, Henri, you will take the leap
   At which so often you have laughed;
You must have taken many a peep
   While Hymen's garden wall you chaffed!

There never was a likely lad
   Who didn't some time want to marry;
I hear you "have it pretty bad"—
   Sly dog, you fetched, now you must carry!

No more late suppers at the club,
   No more the quiet poker party;
You've had your outing — there's the rub —
   You must keep innings now, my hearty!

Henceforth the dear domestic hearth
   Shall light the limits of your vision;
Henceforth your dearest joys on earth
   Be those that once were your derision!

I see you, Henri, walk the floor,
   I hear you groan — it must be colic,
I hear a faint infantile roar —
   Behold your early morning frolic!

A thousand times I wish you joy,
　Bright be the paths where Hymen's beckoned;
Keep a stiff upper lip, my boy,
　And here's a health to Henri II.!

A SEASIDE INCIDENT.

VANDYKE BROWN.

"WHY, Bob, you dear old fellow,
  Where have you been these years?
In Egypt, India, Khiva,
  With the Khan's own volunteers?
Have you scaled the Alps or Andes,
  Sailed to Isles of Amazons?
What climate, Bob, has wrought the change
  Your face from brown to bronze?"

She placed a dimpled hand in mine
  In the same frank, friendly way;
We stood once more on the dear old beach,
  And it seemed but yesterday
Since, standing on this same white shore,
  She said, with eyelids wet,
"Good-bye.   You may remember, Bob,
  But I shall not forget."

I held her hand and whispered low,
  "Madge, darling, what of the years —
The ten long years that have intervened
  Since, through the mist of tears,

We said good-bye on this same white beach
  Here by the murmuring sea ?
You, Madge, were then just twenty,
    And I was twenty-three."

A crimson blush came to her cheek,
  " Hush, Bob," she quickly said ;
" Let's look at the bathers in the surf —
    There's Nellie and Cousin Ned."
" And who's that portly gentleman
    On the shady side of life ? "
" Oh, he belongs to our party, too —
    In fact, Bob, I'm his wife !

" And I tell you, Bob, it's an awful thing,
  The way he does behave :
Flirts with that girl in steel-gray silk —
  Bob, why do you look so grave ? "
" The fact is, Madge — I — well, ahem !
  Oh, nothing at all, my dear —
Except that she of the steel-gray silk
  Is the one I married last year."

HOW A BIBLIOMANIAC BINDS HIS BOOKS

I'D like my favorite books to bind
    So that their outward dress
To every bibliomaniac's mind
    Their contents should express.

Napoleon's life should glare in red,
    John Calvin's gloom in blue ;
Thus they would typify bloodshed
    And sour religion's hue.

The prize-ring record of the past
    Must be in blue and black ;
While any color that is fast
    Would do for Derby track.

The Popes in scarlet well may go
    In jealous green, Othello ;
In gray, Old Age of Cicero,
    And London Cries in yellow

My Walton should his gentle art
    In salmon best express,
And Penn and Fox the friendly heart
    In quiet drab confess.

Statistics of the lumber trade
    Should be embraced in boards ;
While muslin for the inspired Maid
    A fitting garb affords

Intestine wars I'd clothe in vellum,
    While pig-skin Bacon grasps,
And flat romances such as " Pelham,"
    Should stand in calf with clasps.

Blind-tooled should be blank verse and rhyme
    Of Homer and of Milton ;
But Newgate Calendar of Crime
    i'd lavishly dab gilt on.

The edges of a sculptor's life
    May fitly marbled be
But sprinkle not, for fear of strife,
    A Baptist history

Crimea's warlike facts and dates
    Of fragrant Russia smell ;
The subjugated Barbary States
    In crushed Morocco dwell.

But, oh! that one I hold so dear
Should be arrayed so cheap
Gives me a qualm; I sadly fear
My Lamb must be half sheep!

YES?

H. C. BUNNER.

IS it true then, my girl, that you mean it —
  The word spoken yesterday night ?
Does that hour seem so sweet now between it
  And this has come day's sober light ?
Have you woke from a moment of rapture
  To remember, regret, and repent,
And to hate, perchance, him who has trapped your
  Unthinking consent ?

Who was he, last evening — this fellow
  Whose audacity lent him a charm ?
Have you promised to wed Pulchinello
  For life taking Figaro's arm ?
Will you have the Court fool of the papers,
  The clown in the journalists' ring
Who earns his scant bread by his capers,
  To be your heart's king ?

When we met quite by chance at the theater
  And I saw you home under the moon,
I'd no thought, love, that mischief would be at her
  Tricks with my tongue quite so soon ;

23

That I should forget fate and fortune,
   Make a difference 'twixt Sèvres and delf —
That I'd have the calm nerve to importune
   You, sweet, for yourself.

It's appalling, by Jove, the audacious
   Effrontery of that request !
But you — you grew suddenly gracious,
   And hid your sweet face on my breast.
Why you did it I cannot conjecture ;
   I surprised you, poor child, I dare say,
Or perhaps — does the moonlight affect your
   Head often that way ?

You're released !   With some wooer replace me
   More worthy to be your life's light ;
From the tablet of memory efface me,
   If you don't mean the Yes of last night.
But, unless you are anxious to see me a
   Wreck of the pipe and the cup,
In my birthplace and graveyard, Bohemia —
   Love, don't give me up !

SHE WAS A BEAUTY.

(RONDEL.)

H. C. BUNNER.

S HE was a beauty in the days
    When Madison was President ;
And quite coquettish in her ways·—
    On conquests of the heart intent.

Grandpapa, on his right knee bent,
    Wooed her in stiff, old-fashioned phrase —
    She was a beauty in the days
When Madison was President.

And when your roses where hers went
    Shall go, my Rose, who date from Hayes,
I hope you'll wear her sweet content,
    Of whom tradition lightly says :
    She was a beauty in the days
When Madison was President.

JUST A LOVE-LETTER.

H. C. BUNNER.

Miss Blank — at Blank. Jemima, let it go!"—AUSTIN DOBSON.

NEW-YORK, July 20th, 1883

DEAR GIRL:

The town goes on as though
It thought you still were in it;
The gilded cage seems scarce to know
That it has lost its linnet;
The people come, the people pass;
The clock keeps on a-ticking:
And through the basement plots of grass
Persistent weeds are pricking.

I thought 'twould never come—the Spring—
Since you had left the City;
But on the snow-drifts lingering
At last the skies took pity,
Then Summer's yellow warmed the sun,
Daily decreasing distance—
I really don't know how 'twas done
Without your kind assistance.

26

Aunt Van, of course, still holds the fort :
    I've paid the call of duty ;
She gave me one small glass of port —
    'Twas '34 and fruity.
The furniture was draped in gloom
    Of linen brown and wrinkled ;
I smelt in spots about the room
    The pungent camphor sprinkled.

I sat upon the sofa, where
    You sat and dropped your thimble —
You know — you said you didn't care ;
    But I was nobly nimble.
On hands and knees I dropped, and tried
    To — well, tried to miss it :
You slipped your hand down by your side —
    You knew I meant to kiss it !

Aunt Van, I fear we put to shame
    Propriety and precision :
But, praised be Love ! that kiss just came
    Beyond your line of vision.
Dear maiden aunt ! the kiss, more sweet
    Because 'tis surreptitious,
You never stretched a hand to meet,
    So dimpled, dear, delicious.

I sought the Park last Saturday ;
    I found the drive deserted ;
The water-trough beside the way
    Sad and superfluous spurted.

JUST A LOVE-LETTER

I stood where Humboldt guards the gate
   Bronze, bumptious, stained, and streaky—
There sat a sparrow on his pate,
   A sparrow chirp and cheeky.

Ten months ago! ten months ago!—
   It seems a happy second,
Against a life-time lone and slow,
   By Love's wild time-piece reckoned—
You smiled, by Aunt's protecting side,
   Where thick the drags were massing,
On one young man who didn't ride,
   But stood and watched you passing.

I haunt Purssell's—to his amaze—
   Not that I care to eat there;
But for the dear clandestine days
   When we two had to meet there.
Oh! blessed is that baker's bake,
   Past cavil and past question;
I ate a bun for your dear sake,
   And Memory helped Digestion.

The Norths are at their Newport ranch;
   Van Brunt has gone to Venice;
Loomis invites me to the Branch,
   And lures me with lawn-tennis.
O bustling barracks by the sea!
   O spiles, canals, and islands!
Your varied charms are naught to me—
   My heart is in the Highlands!

My paper trembles in the breeze
   That all too faintly flutters
Among the dusty city trees,
   And through my half-closed shutters.
A northern captive in the town,
   Its native vigor deadened,
I hope that, as it wandered down,
   Your dear pale cheek it reddened.

I'll write no more.   A *vis-à-vis*
   In halcyon vacation
Will sure afford a much more free
   Mode of communication;
I'm tantalized and cribbed and checked
   In making love by letter:
I know a style more brief, direct —
   And generally better!

REFUSED

MADELINE S. BRIDGES

"NO, no," she said, and firmly spoke ,
   She reasoned with him like a mother,
And showed why he should be content
   To let her love him as a brother.

She pictured how the marriage state
   Is one of trouble and confusion ;
How love, at best, is but a snare,
   And plainly sent for man's delusion.

He bowed his head before her flow
   Of eloquence, nor strove to turn it,
But meekly hinted that he would
   The lesson take, and try to learn it

" Farewell, I go beyond the sea
   Since I'm refused, no more I'll press you ,
Kind Time," he sighed, " may heal my pain,
   Forgive, forget me, and God bless you ! "

She faltered, paled, then tossed her head :
  " I see it will not greatly grieve you ;
You can't have loved me much," she said :
  " And yet, indeed, I *did* believe you ! "

" Besides," with this her fair cheek gained
  The color his was slowly losing ;
" I only said 'no' once or twice,
  And—women don't call *that* refusing ! "

EVEN UP.

MADELINE S. BRIDGES.

"MY love," he said, and parted back her hair
  That tossed in golden mists above her eyes;
"Ask me no more, but hear me while I swear
  You, you alone I love.   Will that suffice ?

I have had fancies—yes, like other men—
  Youth's blood is swift, and youth's warm dreaming
    roves—
My heart at last is fixed.   Ah ! spare me then
  These questions as to other, earlier loves '

'Tis not for you, whose innocent young heart
  Still hears the music of your childhood's chimes,
To understand   —" She stopped him with a start,
  Don't go so fast, I've been engaged four times ! "

3?

AFTERWARD.

MADELINE S. BRIDGES.

" NEVER," he vowed it, "while life may last,
      Can I love again.   I will die unwed."
" And I, too, dear, since our dream is past,
      I will live single," she sobbing said.

A storm of farewells—of wild good-byes—
      He rushed from the spot, like an outcast soul.
She hid in a pillow her streaming eyes,
      And wept with anguish beyond control.

Just five years afterward, they two met
      At a vender's stand, in a noisy street ;
He saw the smile he could ne'er forget,
      And she the eyes that were more than sweet.

    .

" Oh, Kate ! " " Oh, Harry ! " ⎰ " How well you look."
                              ⎱ " How well you look."
   " I stopped," he said, " just to get a toy
For my little girl."   " I wanted a book,"
   She softly said, " for my little boy."

33

HER LOGIC.

MADELINE S. BRIDGES.

I MAY not kiss you, sweetest? why,
  Since all the world to love is moulded?
Look how the happy butterfly
  Kisses the rose and isn't scolded!

See how the stream with tender lips
  Its green and mossy margin presses,
And even the stately willow dips
  Her beauty to the tide's caresses.

I may not kiss you? 'Tis absurd
  To scorn the truth all nature traces!
The very breeze, upon my word,
  Stands still, and kisses both our faces.

"Quite right," she said, "for breezes, John,
  For butterflies and streamlets, dearest,
I notice, though, they soon pass on
  To kiss—the next thing that comes nearest!'

AN IVORY MINIATURE.

HELEN GRAY CONE.

WHEN State street homes were stately still,
  When out of town was Murray Hill,
In late deceased "old times"
Of vast, embowering bonnet shapes
And creamy-crinkled Canton crapes
  And florid annual rhymes,

He owned a small suburban seat
Where now you see a modern street,
  A monochrome of brown :
The sad "brown brown" of Dante's dreams,
A twilight turned to stone that seems
  To weight our city down.

Through leafy chestnuts whitely showed
The pillared front of his abode :
  A garden girt it 'round,
Where pungent box did trim enclose
The marigold and cabbage rose,
  And "pi'ny" heavy crowned.

Yea, whatso sweets the changing year's,
He most affected. Gone ! but here's

35

His face who loved him so.
Old cheeks like sherry, warm and mild;
A clear-hued cheek as cheek of child;
   Sleek head a sphere of snow.

His mouth was pious, and his nose
Patrician; with which mould there goes
   A disaffected view
In those sublime, be-oratored,
Spread-eagle days; his soul deplored
   So *much* red-white-and-blue!

In umber ink, with S's long,
He left behind him censure strong
   In stiffest phrases clothed!
But time — a pleasant jest enough! —
Has turned the tory leaves to buff,
   The liberal hue he loathed.

Of many a gentle deed he made
Brief, simple record. Never fade
   Those everlasting flowers
That spring up wild by good men's walks;
Opinions wither on their stalks,
   And sere grow Fashion's bowers.

Erect, befrilled, in neckcloth tall,
His semblance sits, removed from all
   Our needs and noises new;
Released from all the rent we pay
As tenants of the large To-day,
   Cool, in a back ground blue.

And he beneath a cherub chipped
Plump, squamous-pinioned, pouting-lipped,
　　Sleeps calm where Trinity
Points fingers dark to clouds that fleet;
A warning, seen from surging street,
　　A welcome seen from sea.

There fall, ghosts glorified of tears
Shed for the dead in buried years,
　　The silver notes of chimes;
And there, with not unreverent hand
Though light, I lay this "greene garland,"
　　This woven wreath of rhymes.

THE BALLAD OF CASSANDRA BROWN.

HELEN GRAY CONE.

THOUGH I met her in the summer, when one's heart
  lies round at ease,
As it were in tennis costume, and a man's not hard to
  please,
Yet I think that any season to have met her was to love,
While her tones, unspoiled, unstudied, had the softness
  of the dove.

At request she read us poems in a nook among the pines,
And her artless voice lent music to the least melodious
    lines ;
Though she lowered her shadowing lashes, in an earnest
    reader's wise,
Yet we caught blue gracious glimpses of the heavens
    which were her eyes.

As in paradise I listened —ah, I did not understand
That a little cloud, no larger than the average human
    hand,
Might, as stated oft in fiction, spread into a sable pall,
When she said that she should study Elocution in the
    fall !

I admit her earliest efforts were not in the Ercles vein;
She began with, " Lit-tle Maaybel, with her faayce against
    the payne
And the beacon-light a-t-r-r-remble"— which, although it
    made me wince,
Is a thing of cheerful nature to the things she's rendered
    since.

Having heard the Soulful Quiver, she acquired the Melt-
    ing Mo-o-an,
And the way she gave "Young Grayhead" would have
    liquefied a stone.
Then the Sanguinary Tragic did her energies employ,
And she tore my taste to tatters when she slew "The
    Polish Boy."

It's not pleasant for a fellow when the jewel of his soul
Wades through slaughter on the carpet, while her orbs
    in frenzy roll;
What was I that I should murmur? Yet it gave me
    grievous pain
That she rose in social gatherings, and Searched among
    the Slain.

I was forced to look upon her in my desperation dumb,
Knowing well that when her awful opportunity was come
She would give us battle, murder, sudden death at very
    least,
As a skeleton of warning, and a blight upon the feast.

Once, ah! once I fell a-dreaming; some one played a
  polonaise
I associated strongly with those happier August days ;
And I mused, "I'll speak this evening," recent pangs
  forgotten quite —
Sudden shrilled a scream of anguish : " Curfew SHALL
  not ring to-night ! "

Ah, that sound was as a curfew, quenching rosy, warm
  romance —
Were it safe to wed a woman one so oft would wish in
  France ?
Oh, as she " cal-limbed " that ladder, swift my mounting
  hope came down,
I am still a single cynic ; she is still Cassandra Brown !

THE MESSAGE OF THE ROSE.

BESSIE CHANDLER.

He.

SHE gave me a rose at the ball to-night,
 And I — I'm a fool, I suppose,
For my heart beat high with a vague delight.
 Had she given me more than the rose?

I thought that she had for a little while
 Till I saw her, fairest of dancers,
Give another rose with the same sweet smile
 To another man in the Lancers.

Well, roses are plenty, and smiles not rare —
 It is really rather audacious
To grumble because my lady fair
 Is to other men kind and gracious.

Yet who can govern his wayward dreams?
 And my dream so precious and bright
Now foolish, broken, and worthless seems
 As it fades with her rose to-night!

She.

I gave him a rose at the ball to-night,
 A deep-red rose, with a fragrance dim,
And the warm blood rushed to my cheeks with fright
 I could not, dared not, look at him.

41

For the depths of my soul he seemed to scan,
    His earnest look I could not bear;
So I gave a rose to another man
    Any one else — I did not care.

And yet, spite of all, he has read, I know,
    My message — he could not have missed it;
For *his* rose I held to my bosom, so,
    And then to my lips while I kissed it.

TO MRS. CARLYLE.

BESSIE CHANDLER.

I HAVE read your glorious letters,
   Where you threw aside all fetters,
     Spoke your thoughts and mind out freely,
        In your own delightful style;
And I fear my state's alarming,
For these pages are so charming
     That my heart I lay before you,—
        Take it, Jeannie Welsh Carlyle.

And I sit here, thinking, thinking
How your life was one long winking
     At poor Thomas' faults and failings
        And his undue share of bile.
Won't you own, dear, just between us,
That this living with a genius
     Isn't after all so pleasant,—
        Is it, Jeannie Welsh Carlyle?

There was nothing so demeaning
In those frequent times of cleaning,
     When you scoured and scrubbed and hammered
        In such true housewifely style,

And those charming teas and dinners,
Graced by clever saints and sinners,
  Make me long to have been present
      With you, Jeannie Welsh Carlyle.

How you fought with dogs and chickens,
Playing children, and the dickens
  Knows what else ; you stilled all racket
      That might Thomas' sleep beguile.
How you wrestled with the taxes,
How you ground T. Carlyle's axes,
  Making him the more dependent
      On you, Jeannie Welsh Carlyle.

Through it all from every quarter
Gleams, like sunshine on the water,
  Your quick sense of fun and humor
      And your bright, bewitching smile.
And I own I fairly revel
In the way that you say "devil,"—
  'Tis so terse, so very vigorous,
      So like Jeannie Welsh Carlyle.

All the time, say, were you missing
Just a little love and kissing —
  Silly things that help to lighten
      Many a weary, dreary while?
Not a word you say to show it,—
We may guess, but never know it,—
  You went quietly on without it,
      Loyal Jeannie Welsh Carlyle.

3*

THE STORK'S JEREMIAD.

BESSIE CHANDLER.

"ONE-LEGGÈD stork, thou standest sad and lonely,
    A tear, methinks, I notice in thine eye.
Oh, tell to me — yes, whisper to me only —
    What is the sorrow that I think I spy?"

And lo! from out the meshes of the tidy
    There came a feeble, mournful sort of squeak.
And, while amazed I opened my eyes wide, he
    Opened his mouth, and thus began to speak: ·

" I am so very tired of being artistic;
    My life is one long, patient, painful ache;
I am so wearied of these weird and mystic
    Positions which they force my form to take.

" In crewels, silks, in worsted and in cotton,
    Now black, now white, now grave, now madly gay,
They've worked me; and one wrong is unforgotten
    They've done me most and worst in appliqué.

"Sometimes they plant me 'mid some rushes speary
    In attitudes no well-bred stork would take,
Holding one leg up, till I get so weary
    I sometimes think my poor strained back will break.

"They've worked me standing, running, sleeping, flying;
    Sometimes I'm gazing at a cruel sun.
They've worked me every way, I think, but dying;
    And oh! I wish they'd do that and be done!

"I could forgive them all this bitter wronging
    If they would grant one favor, which I beg,
Would gratify but once my soul's deep longing,
    Just to put down my cramped and unused leg.

"Know you of any one with sorrows greater?
    A creature with a life that's more forlorn?
Hounded forever by the Decorator,
    I wish, I wish, I never had been born!"

A silence fell; I gazed; he had subsided.
    I listened vainly; all was dumb and still
Upon the tidy where the stork resided,
    With upheld leg and red and open bill.

FOLLY.

BALLARD CRAIG.

PALMS in shadow—a drooping head,
  Crowned by a Folly's cap of red ;
Violet eyes, 'twixt white lids pressed,
Fingers fashioned to be caressed,
A throat that gleams, in the shadows—white,
Lips that tremble and half invite--
And I love her—tenderly—madly ! Yet—
She loves not me—but to coquette !
And she'd probably tremble and droop and pose
For any other fellows she knows !

The shadow of palms—the lamps turned low,
A strain of music—a fountain's flow ;
Tender eyes of darkest brown,
Before whose passion my eyes look down,
Fingers closing over my own,
With a touch that straight to my heart has flown ;
And I love him—love him dearly ! Yet--
He's the most outrageous flirt in our set !
And he looks as tenderly— I suppose,
In the eyes of every girl he knows !

THE FAIR COPY HOLDER

CHARLES H. CRANDALL.

YON window frames her like a saint
  Within some old cathedral rare ,
Perhaps she is not quite so quaint,
  And yet I think her full as fair !

All day she scans the written lines,
  Until the last dull proof is ended.
Calling the various words and signs,
  By which each error may be mended.

An interceding angel, she,
  'Twixt printing press and author's pen
Perhaps she'd find some faults in me !
  Say, maiden, can you not read men ?

Forgive me, gentle girl, but while
  You bravely work, I've been reflecting
That somewhere in this world of guile
  There's some one's life needs your correcting

Methinks 'tis time you tried this art,
  Which makes the world's wide page read better
For love needs proving, heart with heart
  As well as type with written letter.

4*

A SONG FOR THE HICKORY TREE.

CHARLES H. CRANDALL.

I.

A SONG for the hickory tree !
  While the wind is blowing free,
 And the golden leaves and silver nuts
Drop down for you and me !

As we pull the nuggets out
From their crypts with merry shout,
  The air is filled with perfume distilled
From the spices of the South.

A health for the hickory tree !—
Rough-coated, hale and free—
  For its flesh is white and its heart is bright,
And it laughs with you and me !

II.

The squirrel says with a wink,
 "I'd sing a song, I think,
  To the girl who stands with snow-white hands
And eyes that flash and blink.

" Whose flesh is white and strong,
Whose heart is free from wrong,
    And sound and sweet as the nut at her feet,
And better than any song."

So, take the song, my queen,
For a kiss and a philopene !
    'Mid the golden leaves and silver nuts,
I kneel on the carpet green.

IN SWITZERLAND.

W. A. CROFFUT.

A T Chamouny I woke one morn,
   Hearing afar an Alpine horn
      Upon some glacier to the north,
And thought, although it rained forlorn,
      To saunter forth.

There, in the hall, outside a door,
Waiting their owners, on the floor
      I saw two shiny pairs of shoes,
One pair was eights — or, may be, more;
      The other, twos.

I wondered who those gaiters wore
That such a look of courage bore:
      They seemed alert and battle-scarred,
And all their heels were wounded sore
      On mountain shard.

The lofty insteps spurned the ground
As if up high Olympus bound;
      The tireless soles were worn away;
The smooth and taper toes were round
      And *retroussé.*

51

Sudden my envious thought essayed
To count the conquest they had made,
    And all their pilgrimages view;
O'er glen and glacier, gorge and glade,
    My fancy flew.

I saw them thread the Brunig Pass;
I saw them scale the Mer de Glace,
    And Riffleberg, beyond Zermatt;
I saw them mount the mighty mass
    Of Görner Grat.

I saw them climb Bernina's height;
I saw them bathe in Rosa's light
    And linger by the Giessbach Fall;
I saw them grope in Gondo's night
    And Münster Thal;

I saw them find the Jungfrau's head
And leap the Grimsel gorges dread,
    And bound o'er Col de Collon's ice;
And on Belle Tola's summit tread
    The edelweiss.

The vision shamed my listless mood,
Banished my inert lassitude,
    And fired me with intent sublime;
I vowed when sunshine came I would
    Go forth and climb.

With new ambition I arose,
Blessed the foot-gear from heels to toes
    (One pair was eights ; the other, twos),
And thanked the owners brave of those
    Heroic shoes.

IN ARCADIA.

R. T. W. DUKE, JR.

BECAUSE I choose to keep my seat,
    Nor join the giddy dancers' whirl,
I pray you, do not laugh, my girl,
Nor ask me why I find it sweet
    In my old age to watch your glee,—
    I, too, have been in Arcady.

And though full well I know I seem
    Quite out of place in scenes like this,
    You can't imagine how much bliss
It gives me just to sit and dream,
    As you flit by me gracefully,
    How I, too, dwelt in Arcady.

For, sweetheart, in your merry eyes
    A vanished summer buds and blows,
    And with the same bright cheeks of rose
I see your mother's image rise,
    And, o'er a long and weary track,
    My buried boyhood wanders back.

And as with tear-dimmed eyes I cast
    On your sweet form my swimming glance,
    I think your mother used to dance

Just as you do, in that dead past
  Long years ago — yes, fifty-three —
  When I, too, dwelt in Arcady.

And in the music's laughing notes
  I seem to hear old voices ring
  That have been hushed, ah, many a spring;
And round about me faintly floats
  The echo of a melody
  I used to hear in Arcady.

And yonder youth, — nay, do not blush, —
  The boy's his father o'er again;
  And hark ye, miss ! I was not plain
When at his age — what! must I hush ?
  He's coming this way ? Yes, I see, —
  You two yet dwell in Arcady.

AN OLD BACHELOR TO AN OLD MAID.

MARGARET EYTINGE.

IN early spring the song-birds sing,
  This is Love's season.   Soon shall spread
   A carpet green before his feet,
And crocuses and snowdrops bring
A wreath to crown his lovely head.
   This is Love's season,— sweet, sweet, sweet!

Then, youths and maidens, while ye may,
Your sweethearts choose before the light
   That shines on springtime shall retreat.
For, once that light has passed away,
Life knows again no hours so bright,
   So full of gladness,— sweet, sweet, sweet.

Now, I believe the birds are wrong,—
That is, not altogether right,—
   Love may with partial eyes behold
The spring, but yet, the whole year long
He smiles with tenderest delight
   On all true lovers, young and old.

And though your early summer's fled,
And though my autumn's almost here,
   The lilies, blessed with love divine,
Shall take the place of roses dead.
Will you consent to pluck them, dear,
   With me, and be my valentine?

RONDEL

ANNA MARIA FAY.

WHEN love is in her eyes
    What need of spring for me?
A brighter emerald lies
    On hill and vale and lea

The azure of the skies
    Holds naught so sweet to me :
When love is in her eyes
    What need of spring for me?

Her bloom the rose outvies,
    The lily dares no plea.
The violet's glory dies
    No flower so sweet can be ;
When love is in her eyes
    What need of spring for me?

BALLADE OF THE ROSE.

H. C. FAULKNER.

TELL me, red rose, what you were bid,—
   You know her secret; you she wore
Shy, nestling in her hair, half hid
   By jealous golden curls a score,
    As waves half timid kiss the shore,
Then tremble were they bold or no;
   I kiss you, blushing token, for
She loves me,— rose, you tell me so.

I softly raise your scented lid,
   Where, sleeping since some dawn of yore,
A crystal dewdrop lies amid
   The downy crimson of your core.
    I am not versed in Cupid's lore;
But so I think her blushing glow
   Soft guards the love I sue her for.
She loves me,— rose, you tell me so.

58

And when her hand, in dainty kid,
  Gave you to me, as ne'er before
It fluttered, tried itself to rid
  Of fetters that it never wore,
  Why trembled she ?   My eyes would pour
My love in hers,— why did she so ?
  Was it because she hates me, or —
She loves me,— rose, you tell me so.

L'ENVOY.

Rose, come you not ambassador
  From Cupid's court, to let me know
Love yields at last ?   Speak, I implore !
  She loves me,— rose, you tell me so.

BETWEEN THE LINES.

H. C. FAULKNER.

"*DEAR MR. BROWN,*"— I know she meant
    "Dear Jack"; that D with sentiment
      Is overweighted.
Shy little love! she did not dare;
That flutter in the M shows where
      She hesitated.

The darling girl! what loving heed
She gives the strokes; it does not need
      Great penetration
To note the lingering, trusting touch;
As if to write to me were such
      A consolation.

"*The flowers came; so kind of you.*
A thousand thanks!"   Oh, fie! Miss Prue,
      The line betrays you.
You know just there you sent a kiss;
You meant that blot to tell me this,
      And it obeys you.

"*They gave me such a happy day.*
I love them so.   She meant to say,
      "Because you sent them."

But then, you see, the page is small;
She wrote in haste — the words — and all,—
    I know she *meant* them.

" *At night I kept them near me, too,*
And dreamt of them," she wrote, " and you,"
    But would erase it.
Did she but have one tender thought
That perished with the blush it brought,
    My love would trace it.

" *This morning all the buds have blown.*"
That flourish surely is " Your own ; "
    'Tis written queerly ;
She meant it so.   Ah, useless task
To hide your love 'neath such a mask
    As that " Sincerely."

" *Prudence.*"   Those tender words confess
As much to me as a caress ;
    And, Prue, you know it.
But then, to tease me, you must add
Your other name, although you had
    Scarce space to do it.

A dash prolonged across the sheet
To close the note ? — the little cheat,—
    No.   When she penned it
She meant its quavering length to say
That she could write to me for aye,
    And never end it.

True! Love is like the flame that glows
Unseen till, lightly fanned, it grows
    Too fierce to quell it.
And mine! Ah, mine is unconfessed;
But now,—that dash and all the rest,—
    I'll have to tell it.

BALLADE OF THE BALCONY

H. C. FAULKNER.

He.

CHEEKS that are *shirato* white,
  Eyes that are deep *nankin* blue,
Heart that I fear me is quite
  Hardened as porcelain too.

She.

Antique, of course, and a fright!
  Porcelain never is new.

He.

I know this passionless sprite,
  Sweet Miss Thalia; do you?
Fickle as May ——

She.

      And as bright?

He.

Dances each night until two,
  Flirts on the lake by moonlight.

She.

Some one must row the canoe.
  Ah, lovely empress of night!
Maidens must worship thee ——

He.
Pooh !

I hardly think this is right,
Sweet Miss Thalia ; do you ?

She.
But, if it give her delight ?
Lovers are sadly too few.

He.
Yet, if she loved a poor wight,
One, I should fancy, would do.

She.
Yes ; but is not the bold knight
Sometimes a laggard to woo ?

He.
Think you she loves him a mite,
Sweet Miss Thalia ; do you ?

L'ENVOY.

She.
Pray, sir ! your arms are too tight '

He.
Knights kissed their lady-loves true.

She.
Then I think — mayhap — you — might —

He.
Sweet Miss Thalia, do you ?

THE GAME OF CHESS.

DAVID S. FOSTER.

'TWAS stinging, blustering, winter weather;
  How well I recollect the night!
When Kate and I played chess together.
  Her beauty in the hearth-fire's light
Seemed more Madonna-like and rosy ;
The hours were swift, the room was cozy,
  The windows frosted silvery white.

Even now I see that grave face resting
  Upon the hand, so white and small ;
I see that mystic grace, suggesting
  A painter's dream ; I oft recall
Her glance, now anxious, gay, or tender ;
The girlish form, complete yet slender,
  In silhouette against the wall.

It was not strange that I was mated,
  For 'twas my fondly cherished aim.
I longed to speak, but I was fated ;
  The rightful opening never came.
I pawned my heart for her sweet favor,
With every look some vantage gave her,
  An so, alas ! I lost the game.

85

Since then, by fortune, love, forsaken,
  Through checkered years I've passed and seen
My castles fall, my pawns all taken,
  My spotless knights prove traitors mean ;
And worn with many a check, I wander
Like the poor vanquished king, and ponder
  With sadness on my long-lost queen.

AFTER THE BALL.

MINNIE GILMORE.

OH, little glove, do I but dream I hold thee,
 So warm, so sweet, and tawny as her hair?
Nay! from her hand I dared unfold thee,
 As we went down the stair.

She said no word; she did not praise nor blame me;
 She is so proud, so proud and cold and fair!
Ah! dear my love, thy silence did not shame me
 As we went down the stair.

Thy dark eyes flashed; thy regal robes arrayed thee
 In queenly grace, and pride beyond compare;
But on thy cheek a sudden red betrayed thee,
 As we went down the stair.

O lady mine, some near night will I prove thee!
 By this soft glove I know that I may dare
Take thy white hand and whisper, "Sweet, I love thee,"
 As we go down the stair.

A LOST FRIEND.

MINNIE GILMORE.

YOUR soul, that for years I have counted
  An open book, read to the end,
Is lettered all strange, since a lover
  Looks out from the eyes of a friend.

The white pages now are turned rosy,
  The chapters are numbered anew,
The old plot is lost, and the hero
  Who, up to last night, was just you —

Just dear old friend Jack, and no other,
  To-night is a stranger, I vow;
And though I am fain to be gracious,
  The truth is, I scarcely know how.

Where now is your celibate gospel?
  What now of Love's follies and faults?
Refuted last night when your lips, sir,
  Chasséed o'er my cheek in the waltz.

Life-faith we swore, friendly fraternal
  To keep it — ah me! half a year

6

And I, Chloris now to your Strephon,
   Accept my new rôle with a tear,—

A tear for the dear old days ended,
   A tear for the friend lost for aye,
For careless old comradeship fleeing
   Forever before Love to-day.

Dear, read me aright! Though words falter,
   And lips prove but dumb, your heart hears ;
The Jack of to-day I love truly,
   Yet oh for the Jack of old years !

RONDEAUX OF CITIES.

ROBERT GRANT.

I.

RONDEAU À LA BOSTON.

A CULTURED mind! Before I speak
The words, sweet maid, to tinge thy cheek
With blushes of the nodding rose
That on thy breast in beauty blows,
I prithee satisfy my freak.

Canst thou read Latin and eke Greek?
Dost thou for knowledge pine and peek?
Hast thou, in short, as I suppose,
    A cultured mind?

Some men require a maiden meek
Enough to eat at need the leek;
Some lovers crave a classic nose,
A liquid eye, or faultless pose;
I none of these. I only seek
    A cultured mind.

5

II.

A pedigree! Ah, lovely jade!
Whose tresses mock the raven's shade,
   Before I free this aching breast
   I want to set my mind at rest;
'Tis best to call a spade a spade.

What was thy father ere he made
His fortune? Was he smeared with trade,
   Or does he boast an ancient crest —
      A pedigree?

Brains and bright eyes are over-weighed;
For wits grow dull and beauties fade;
   And riches, though a welcome guest,
   Oft jar the matrimonial nest.
I kiss her lips who holds displayed
      A pedigree.

III.

RONDEAU À LA BALTIMORE.

A PRETTY face! O maid divine,
Whose vowels flow as soft as wine,
   Before I say upon the rack
   The words I never can take back,
A moment meet my glance with thine.

Say, art thou fair? Is the incline
Of that sweet nose an aquiline?
   Hast thou, despite unkind attack,
            A pretty face?

Some sigh for wisdom. Three, not nine,
The graces were. I won't repine
   For want of pedigree, or lack
   Of gold to banish Care the black,
If I can call forever mine
            A pretty face.

IV.

A POT of gold!   O mistress fair,
With eyes of brown that pass compare,
  Ere I on bended knee express
  The love which you already guess,
I fain would ask a small affair.

Hast thou, my dear, an ample share
Of this world's goods?   Will thy proud père
  Disgorge, to gild our blessedness,
          A pot of gold?

Some swains for mental graces care;
Some fall a prey to golden hair;
  I am not blind, I will confess,
  To intellect or comeliness;
Still let these go beside, *ma chère*,
          A pot of gold.

PRIVATE THEATRICALS.

LOUISE IMOGENE GUINEY.

YOU were a haughty beauty, Polly,
    (That was in the play,)
I was the lover melancholy,
    (That was in the play.)
And when your fan and you receded,
And all my passion lay unheeded,
If still with tenderer words I pleaded,
    That was in the play !

I met my rival at the gateway,
    (That was in the play,)
And so we fought a duel straightway,
    (That was in the play.)
But when Jack hurt my arm unduly,
And you rushed over, softened newly,
And kissed me, Polly ! truly, truly,
    Was that in the play ?

LO AND LU.

LOUISE IMOGENE GUINEY.

WHEN we began this never-ended,
  Kind companionship,
Childish greetings lit the splendid
  Laughter at the lip;
You were ten and I eleven;
  Henceforth, as we knew,
Was all mischief under heaven
  Set down to Lo and Lu.

Long we fought and cooed together,
  Held an equal reign,
Snowballs could we fire and gather,
  Twine a clover chain;
Sing in G an A flat chorus
  'Mid the tuneful crew —
No harmonious angels o'er us
  Taught us, Lo or Lu.

Pleasant studious times have seen us
  Arm in arm of yore,
Learned books, well thumbed between us,
  Spread along the floor;

75

Perched in pine tops, sunk in barley,
 Rogues where rogues were few,
Right or wrong in deed or parley,
 Comrades, Lo and Lu.

Which could leap where banks were wider,
 Mock the cat-bird's call?
Which preside and pop the cider
 At a festival?
Who became the finer stoic,
 Stabbing trouble through,
Thrilled to hear of things heroic
 Oftener, Lo or Lu?

Earliest, blithest! then and ever
 Mirror of my heart!
Grow we old and wise and clever
 Now, so far apart;
Still as tender as a mother's
 Floats our prayer for two;
Neither yet can spare the other's
 " God bless — Lo and Lu! "

BALLADE OF THE SHEPHERDESS.

(IRREGULAR.)

RUTH HALL.

IN the dazzling blue and white of the tiles
　As a mirror my dear love's face I spy;
From the mantel tree she looks down and smiles,
　While my heart goes up in an answering sigh.
　It's I am so lowly and she is so high,
My bashful hope how could I confess,
　But an English pug, and yet dare to cry
For the love of a china shepherdess?

She leans on the crook — oh, her winning wiles!
　From my mistress' lap, where I idly lie,
I watch, and I wish there were miles and miles
　(While my heart goes up in an answering sigh)
　'Twixt her and that boy with the butterfly.
So pretty is he in his peasant dress,
　And so plain beside him, how should I try
For the love of a china shepherdess?

BALLADE OF THE SHEPHERDESS.

There's an Angora cat my bark reviles,
   Did I love, mayhap she would make reply;
But no! to the mantel tree's dim defiles
    (While my heart goes up in an answering sigh)
   All possible bliss must pass me by,
And no one shall ever the secret guess :
   An unlucky dog is in misery
For love of a china shepherdess.

L'ENVOY.

Ah, many a wight of more wit than I
Is dying to live and living to die —
Would give up his heart and his soul — no less
For love of a china shepherdess !

WINTER'S WOOING.

RUTH HALL.

DEAR heart of mine, true heart of mine,
 'Tis time o' year for valentine;
Grim Winter doth his silence break
Now, love to make, for April's sake;
Wild flow'rs entreat her face to greet
When she shall come and make all sweet
Before the light touch of her feet.

Dear heart of mine, own heart of mine,
Ah, well may Winter loud repine!
She turns before her suitor bold:
He is so old, he is so cold —
No! dear is May, and near is May,
He cannot, now, be far away,
And so she says old Winter, Nay.

Dear heart of mine, sweet heart of mine,
Shall love meet love and make no sign?
The weeks they come, the weeks they go;
Nor Winter's snow nor Summer's glow
Can chill the land, can thrill the land,
As look of eye and touch of hand
May those true souls who *understand!*

TOO LEARNED.

RUTH HALL.

MA says I am lucky as I can be
  To marry Professor Gaunt,
And Pa says he wonders what he can see
  In a girl like me to want;
And at first no one was prouder than I
  (His fame is world-wide, you know),
But — I must tell some one or I shall die -
  Nell, it is awfully slow.

I thought he'd come wooing like other men,
  In spite of being so wise,
And say he loved me again and again,
  And praise my hair and my eyes.
But he talks of things I can't understand,
  Of fossils and snakes and shells;
He never dreams of holding my hand,
  Or bringing me caramels.

I want a lover to talk of love,
  Smooth my hair and look at me;
I want him to call me "Darling" and "Dove,"
  And pull me down on his knee;
I want him to write me foolish rhymes,
  To give me some little surprise :
Well, I can't help it, I wish sometimes
  He wasn't so awfully wise!

MRS. GOLIGHTLY.

GERTRUDE HALL.

THE time is come to speak, I think;
    For on the square I met
My beauteous widow, fresh and pink,
Her black gown touched at every brink
    With tender violet.

And at her throat the white *crêpe lisse*
    Spoke in a fluffy bow
Of woe that should perhaps ne'er cease,
(Peace to thy shade, Golightly, peace!)
    Yet mitigated woe.

In her soft eye, that used to scan
    The ground, nor seem to see,
The hazel legend sweetly ran,
" I *could* not wholly hate a man
    For quite adoring me."

And when she drew her 'kerchief fine,
    A hint of heliotrope
Its snow, edged with an inky line,
Exhaled — from which scent you divine
    Through old regrets new hope.

And then her step — so soft and slow,
    She scarcely seemed to lift

From off the sward her widowed toe,
One year — one little year ago! —
   So soft yet, yet so swift ;

Then, too, her blush, her side glance coy,
   Tell me in easy Greek,—
(I wonder could her little boy
Prove source of serious annoy ?)
   The time is come to speak.

ALNASCHAR — NEW-YORK, 1887.

MRS. M. P. HANDY.

WHERE was I last week? At the Skinners';
 It's really a nice place to dine:
The old man gives capital dinners,
 And is rather a good judge of wine.
The daughters are stylish and pretty
 Nice girls! eh? Don't know them, you say?
Indeed! That is really a pity;
 I'll take you there with me some day.

You'll be pleased with the eldest — Miss Carrie;
 But Maude's rather more in my style.
By George! if a fellow could marry,
 There's a girl who would make it worth while!
But it costs such a lot when you're doubled;
 You must live in some style,—there's the rub.
Now, a single man isn't so troubled,
 It's always good form at the club.

As to Maude, she'd say yes in a minute,
 If I asked for her hand, I dare say:
Soft, white hand,— if a fortune were in it,
 I'd ask her to have me to-day.

4

Father rich ? Well, you know there's no knowing
  How a man will cut up till he's dead.
Have I looked at his tax-list? I'm going
  To do it; old boy, that's well said !

But even rich fathers aren't willing
  Always to come down with the pelf;
They'll say they began with a shilling,
  And think you can do it yourself.
What's that paper, just there ? The *Home Journal!*
  What's the news in society, eh ?
ENGAGED ! Now, by all the infernal —
  It can't be ; pass it over this way.

Hm ! " Reception, Club breakfast, Grand dinner,
  " We learn that the charming Miss Maude,
Youngest daughter of Thomas O. Skinner,
  Is engaged to George Jones,"— He's a fraud !—
" Of the firm of Jones, Skinner & Baker,
  The marriage will take place in May."
Hang the girl for a flirt, the deuce take her !
  Well, what are you laughing at, eh ?

DE CONVENANCE.

MRS. M. P. HANDY.

SO glad you are here for the wedding!
   I want you to see my trousseau.
Pa gave me *carte blanche* for the outfit,—
   'Tis all he need give me, you know.
'Tisn't every girl marries three millions,
   And so he's as pleased as can be.
Here's the dress dear, white satin, Worth's latest,
   And the flounces and veil real point : see !

The girls are all dying with envy.
   Last summer at Newport, the way
They courted the man for his money
   Was disgusting, I really must say.
Oh, Tiffany's keeping my diamonds —
   I shouldn't feel safe with them here ;
I think they will make a sensation ;
   No bride has had finer this year.

Of course we are going to Europe,
   The state-rooms are taken and all ;
How long we shall stay I don't know, but
   I guess until late in the fall.

When we get back, I'll give a grand party.
   The house he is building up town
Will be something superb when it's finished;
   I wish the man's name wasn't Brown!

In love with him?   Jule! why, you're joking;
   He's fifty at least, if a day;
But then, he is really in love, dear,—
   I'm sure I shall have my own way.
You know I was never romantic;
   If he wants a pretty young wife,
Why, I don't object to be petted
   And worshiped the rest of my life.

It's wicked to marry for money?
   Oh, yes, but who likes being poor?
Don't they say love flies out of the window
   When poverty darkens the door?
I did come near falling in love once
   With the handsomest fellow in town,
An artist, with nothing but talent —
   My stars! how the pater did frown!

But now he's delighted.   Three millions!
   What well-brought-up girl dare refuse?
And the other girls' mothers are wishing
   Their own daughters stood in my shoes.
There's my *fiancé* now.   See his horses!
   Perhaps he does look rather grim.
And what of the other young artist?
   Ah, well, we won't talk about him!

A CHALLENGE.

JAMES CLARENCE HARVEY.

"GOOD-night," he said, and he held her hand,
  In a hesitating way,
And hoped that her eyes would understand
  What his tongue refused to say.

He held her hand and he murmured low :
  "I'm sorry to go like this.
It seems so frigidly cool, you know,
  This 'Mister' of ours, and 'Miss.'"

"I thought—perchance"—and he paused to note
  If she seemed inclined to frown ;
But the light in her eyes his heartstrings smote,
  As she blushingly looked down.

She spoke no word, but she picked a speck
  Of dust from his coat lapel ;
So small, such a wee, little, tiny fleck,
  'Twas a wonder she saw so well.

But it brought her face so very near,
  In that dim, uncertain light,
That the thought, unspoken, was made quite clear,
  And I know 'twas a sweet "Good-night."

HALF AN HOUR BEFORE SUPPER.

BRET HARTE.

" SO she's here, your unknown Dulcinea—the lady
    you met on the train—
And you really believe she would know you if you were
    to meet her again ? "

" Of course," he replied. " she would know me ; there
    never was womankind yet
Forgot the effect she inspired.   She excuses, but does
    not forget."

" Then you told her your love ? " asked the elder ; the
    younger looked up with a smile :
" I sat by her side half an hour—what else was I doing
    the while ?

" What, sit by the side of a woman as fair as the sun in
    the sky,
And look somewhere else lest the dazzle flash back
    from your own to her eye ?

" No, I hold that the speech of the tongue be as frank
    and as bold as the look,
And I held up herself to herself—that was more than
    she got from the book."

" Young blood ! " laughed the elder ; " no doubt you
are voicing the mode of to-day ;
But then we old fogies at least gave the lady some
chance for delay.

" There's my wife—(you must know)—we first met on
the journey from Florence to Rome :
It took me three weeks to discover who was she and
where was her home !

" Three more to be duly presented ; three more ere I
saw her again ;
And a year ere my romance *began* where yours ended
that day in the train."

" Oh, that was the style of the stage coach ; we travel
to-day by express ;
Forty miles to the hour," he answered. "won't admit
of a passion that's less."

" But what if you make a mistake ? " quoth the elder.
The younger half sighed :
"What happens when signals are wrong or switches
misplaced ? " he replied.

"Very well, I must bow to your wisdom," the elder
returned, " but submit
Your chances of winning this woman your boldness has
bettered no whit.

" Why, you do not at best know her name, and what if
     I try your ideal
With something, if not quite so fair, at least more *en
     règle* and real ?

" Let me find you a partner. Nay, come, i insist—
     you shall follow—this way.
My dear, will you not add your grace to entreat Mr.
     Rapid to stay ?

' My wife, Mr. Rapid—Eh, what ! Why, he's gone
     yet he said he would come ;
How rude ! I don't wonder, my dear, you are
     properly crimson and dumb !"

WHAT THE WOLF REALLY SAID TO LITTLE RED RIDING-HOOD.

BRET HARTE.

WONDERING Maiden, so puzzled and fair,
Why dost thou murmur and ponder and stare?
" Why are my eyelids so open and wild? "—
Only the better to see with, my child !
Only the better and clearer to view
Cheeks that are rosy and eyes that are blue.

Dost thou still wonder and ask why these arms
Fill thy soft bosom with tender alarms,
Swaying so wickedly?——are they misplaced
Clasping or shielding some delicate waist?—
Hands whose coarse sinews may fill you with fear,
Only the better protect you, my dear !

Little Red Riding-Hood, when in the street,
Why do I press your small hand when we meet?
Why, when you timidly offer your cheek,
Why did I sigh, and why didn't I speak?
Why, well, you—see if the truth must appear——
I'm not your grandmother, Riding-Hood, dear !

A BOUTONNIÈRE.

CHARLES HENRY LÜDERS.

A DEWY fragrance drifts at times
　　Across my willing senses,
And leads the rillet of my rhymes
From city gutters, gusts, and grimes
　　To lowland fields and fences.

I seem to see, as I inhale
　　This perfume faint and fleeting,
Green hillsides sloping to a vale,
Whose leafy shadows screen the pale
　　Wood-flowers from noonday's greeting.

I hear the song — the sweet heartache —
　　Of just a pair of thrushes;
And hear, half dreaming, half awake,
The ripple of a streamlet break
　　Their momentary hushes.

And why, dear heart, do I to-day,
　　Hemmed in by court and alley,
Seem lost in haunts of faun and fay?
Look! — on my coat I've pinned your spray
　　Of lilies of the valley.

ON A HYMN BOOK.

W. J. HENDERSON.

OLD Hymn Book, sure I thought I'd lo : you
In the days now long gone by ;
I'd forgotten where I tossed you ;
Gracious ! how I sigh.

In the church a thin partition
Stood between her pew and mine ;
And her pious, sweet contrition
Struck me as divine.

Yes, remarkably entrancing
Was she in her sable furs ;
And my eyes were always glancing
Up, old book, to hers.

Bless you, very well she knew it,
And I'm sure she liked it too ;
Once she whispered "Please don't do it,"
But her eyes said "Do."

How to speak—to tell my passion ?
    How to make her think me true ?
Love soon found a curious fashion,
    For he spoke through you.

How I used to search your pages
    For the words I wished to say :
And receive my labor's wages
    Every Sabbath day !

Ah, how sweet it was to hand her
    You, with lines I'd marked when found !
And how well I'd understand her
    When she blushed and frowned !

And one day, old book, you wriggled
    From my hand and, rattling, fell
Upon the floor ; and she—she giggled—
    Did Miss Isabel.

Then when next we met out walking,
    I was told in tearful tones
How she'd get a dreadful talking
    From the Reverend Jones.

Ah me ! No one could resist her
    In those sweet and buried years ;
So I think—I think I kissed her,
    Just to stop her tears.

Jones I gave a good sound chaffing :
  Called his sermon dry as bones ;
Soon fair Isabel was laughing——
  Said she hated Jones.

It was after that I lost you
  For I needed you no more ;
Somewhere—anywhere I tossed you ;
  On a closet floor.

Reverend Samuel still preaches :
  Isabel her past atones.
In his Sunday school she teaches—
  Mrs. Samuel Jones.

PALMISTRY.

W. J. HENDERSON.

OH, give me, Eve, that lily hand —
   Nay, start not with that sudden glow ·
See, palmistry I understand ;
   I'll read these lines before I go.

This head-line's full and broad and long ;
   I know by that to thought you're wed,
And carry culture rich and strong
   Within that graceful, gold-crown'd head.

This line of life is straight and deep :
   By that I know your future's fair ·
Some happiness shall wake from sleep
   To light your life with blessings rare

This heart-line is so true — ah, well.
   One knows that looking in your face
And in your eyes, that truly tell
   How rich the heart must be in grace.

Nay, more I dare not tell, I vow :
   I can't — perhaps you may divine —
But don't you think, pray tell me, now,
   Your hand fits very well in mine ?

MY AUNT

OLIVER WENDELL HOLMES.

MY aunt ! my dear unmarried aunt !
   Long years have o'er her flown ;
Yet still she strains the aching clasp
   That binds her virgin zone ;
I know it hurts her—though she looks
   As cheerful as she can ;
Her waist is ampler than her life,
   For life is but a span.

My aunt ! my poor deluded aunt !
   Her hair is almost gray ;
Why will she train that winter curl
   In such a spring-like way ?
How can she lay her glasses down
   And say she reads as well,
When, through a double convex lens,
   She just makes out to spell ?

Her father—grandpapa ! forgive
  This erring lip its smiles—
Vowed she should make the finest girl
  Within a hundred miles ;
He sent her to a stylish school ;
  'Twas in her thirteenth June ;
And with her, as the rules required,
    " Two towels and a spoon."

They braced my aunt against a board.
  To make her straight and tall ;
They laced her up, they starved her down,
  To make her light and small ;
They pinched her feet, they singed her hair,
  They screwed it up with pins :—
Oh, never mortal suffered more
  In penance for her sins.

So, when my precious aunt was done
  My grandsire brought her back ;
(By daylight, lest some rabid youth
  Might follow on the track)
" Ah ! " said my grandsire, as he shook
  Some powder in his pan,
" What could this lovely creature do
  Against a desperate man ! "

Alas ! nor chariot, nor barouche,
  Nor bandit cavalcade,

Tore from the trembling father's arms
 His all-accomplished maid,
For her how happy had it been !
 And Heaven had spared to me
To see one sad, ungathered rose
 On my ancestral tree.

TO THE PORTRAIT OF "A LADY."

OLIVER WENDELL HOLMES.

WELL, Miss, I wonder where you live,
   I wonder what's your name.
I wonder how you came to be
   In such a stylish frame ;
Perhaps you were a favorite child,
   Perhaps an only one :
Perhaps your friends were not aware
   You had your portrait done !

Yet you must be a harmless soul ;
   I cannot think that Sin
Would care to throw his loaded dice,
   With such a stake to win :
I cannot think you would provoke
   The poet's wicked pen,
Or make young women bite their lips,
   Or ruin fine young men.

Pray, did you ever hear, my love,
   Of boys that go about
Who, for a very trifling sum
   Will snip one's picture out ?

I'm not averse to red and white,
   But all things have their place .
I think a profile cut in black
   Would suit your style of face !

I love sweet features ; I will own
   That I should like myself
To see my portrait on a wall,
   Or bust upon a shelf ;
But nature sometimes makes one up
   Of such sad odds and ends.
It really might be quite as well
   Hushed up among one's friends!

AUNT TABITHA.

OLIVER WENDELL HOLMES

WHATEVER I do, and whatever I say,
  Aunt Tabitha tells me that isn't the way :
When *she* was a girl (forty summers ago)
Aunt Tabitha tells me they never did so.

Dear aunt ! if I only could take her advice !
But I like my own way, and I find it so nice !
And besides, I forget half the things I am told ;
But they all will come back to me—when I am old.

If a youth passes by, it may happen, no doubt.
He may chance to look in as I chance to look out ;
She would never endure an impertinent stare—
It is *horrid* she says, and I mustn't sit there.

A walk in the moonlight has pleasures, I own,
But it isn't quite safe to be walking alone;
So I take a lad's arm—just for safety, you know—
But Aunt Tabitha tells me *they* never did so.

How wicked we are, and how good they were then !
They kept at arm's length those detestable men :
What an era of virtue she lived in—but stay—
Were the *men* all such rogues in Aunt Tabitha's day ?

If the men were so wicked I'll ask my papa
How he dared to propose to my darling mamma ;
Was he like the rest of them? Goodness! Who knows ?
And what shall *I* say if a wretch should propose?

I am thinking if Aunt knew so little of sin,
What a wonder Aunt Tabitha's aunt must have been !
And her grand-aunt—it scares me—how shockingly sad
That we girls of to-day are so frightfully bad !

A martyr will save us, and nothing else can—
Let *me* perish—to rescue some wretched young man !
Though when to the altar a victim I go,
Aunt Tabitha'll tell me *she* never did so !

HEART AND HAND.

CHARLES LOTIN HILDRETH.

SWEET, let me read that little palm ;
  Perchance 'tis true, as sages say,
That there is written many a charm
  To draw the future's veil away.

I press the dainty finger-tips—
  'Tis a preliminary part ;
And hold them softly to my lips—
  Tis a requirement of the art.

Here runs the life line, long and deep ;
  Few crosses on its snowy plain :
Ah, seldom, sweet one, may'st thou weep,
  And seldom know the touch of pain !

And here the line of wealth I see,
  Lost in a broader line above ;
If I know aught that line should be
  The sign of true and perfect love.

Ay, full across the palm it curves,
  And side by side with life it tends ;
It never falters, never swerves,
  And only with the life it ends.

And here another humbler line !
  'Tis that of one who loves thee dear :
See how it followeth close to thine,
  Yet dareth not approach too near !

Yet, stay ! they touch—thy line with his-
  Look where the fateful symbols meet !
Sure that conjunction means a kiss !
  Oh, haste, fulfil the omen, sweet !

ONE OF THE PACK.

GEORGE PARSONS LATHROP.

I SEE how it is . I'm one of the pack.
 A paltry playing card, nothing more :
You shuffle and deal, then take me back,
 Or toss me to lie where I was before.
There are royal heads at your mimic court,
 But they fare no better; they're in the same fix ;
For you vary the usual order of sport :
 You take what you please while you play your tricks.

No doubt it serves well as a source of fun
 To match your lovers, this one against that ;
Though perhaps when the evening's amusement is done
 And the pack put aside, we seem rather flat.
But suppose that by chance in the dead of the night,
 When you dream with disdain of our being inert,
We should break your repose, rising up in our might,
 And declare to your face that our feelings are hurt ?

For, whatever you fancy, we each have a soul.
　And the rules that apply here are oddly so planned
That while we seem bent to your fingers's control
　And are played with, yet we too are taking a hand
Don't you see what a sequence of hearts you may break
　While attempting one mean little trump spot to save ?
Or succumb to an equally luckless mistake
　And let a king go for the sake of a knave ?

Does Tom's diamond take you, or is it my heart ?
　The deuce, after all will perhaps end the race ;
Then again, you may yield to young Algernon Smart,
　Or the one-eyed old banker's Cyclopean ace.
The game's to be Lottery--so you said--
　Or Matrimony ?　No ! both, I declare,
Why, the next thing I know you'll take to old maid
　And leave *me* to sorrow and Solitaire.

Cross purposes still !　This never will do.
　You've began Vingt-et-un ; *I'm* at thirty-one—
Just ten years apart.　Oh, I wish I knew
　Some smoother way to make matters run !
You change the game like a pantomime
　And now its euchre, I really believe,
For you're trying to cheat me half of the time
　With a " little joker "—a laugh in your sleeve.

Let us end this nonsense !　What do you say ?
　Leave me out and go on with the rest,

Or throw the whole heap of cards away,
    And stake your all on a man as the best.
You can't manage love according to Hoyle,
    And your effort to do so you surely would rue :
Besides what's the use of such intricate toil,
    You shall win all the games if I only win you !

LAST JULY.

SOPHIE ST. G. LAWRENCE.

SHE'S barely twenty, and her eyes
    Are very soft and very blue;
Her lips seem made for sweet replies,—
    Perhaps they're made for kisses too;
Her little teeth are white as pearl,
    Her nose aspires to the sky;
She really is a charming girl,
    And I adored her — last July.

We danced and swam, and bowled and walked;
    She let me squeeze her finger tips;
Entranced I listened when she talked,
    And trash seemed wisdom from her lips.
I sent her roses till my purse
    Was drained, I found, completely dry;
I longed to sing her charms in verse —
    But all of this was last July.

Of course at last we had to part;
    I saw a tear drop on her cheek;
I left her with an aching heart,
    And dreamt about her — for a week.

But out of sight is out of mind,
  And somehow, as the time went by,
Much fainter I began to find
  The memory of that last July.

July has come again at last;
  With summer gowns the rocks are gay;
It seemed an echo of the past
  To meet her on the rocks to-day.
She's even fairer than of yore,
  And — yet I could not tell you why —
I find the girl an awful bore —
  So long it is since last July.

TIME'S REVENGE.

WALTER LEARNED.

W HEN I was ten and she fifteen —
    Ah me, how fair I thought her!
She treated with disdainful mien
    The homage that I brought her,
And, in a patronizing way
Would of my shy advances say:
    " It's really quite absurd, you see ;
    He's very much too young for me."

I'm twenty now; she, twenty-five —
    Well, well, how old she's growing!
I fancy that my suit might thrive
    If pressed again ; but, owing
To great discrepancy in age,
Her marked attentions don't engage
    My young affections, for, you see,
    She's really quite too old for me.

ON THE FLY-LEAF
OF A BOOK OF OLD PLAYS.

WALTER LEARNED.

A T Cato's Head in Russell street
These leaves she sat a-stitching;
I fancy she was trim and neat,
Blue-eyed and quite bewitching.

Before her in the street below,
All powder, ruffs, and laces,
There strutted idle London beaux
To ogle pretty faces;

While, filling many a Sedan chair
With hoop and monstrous feather,
In patch and powder London's fair
Went trooping past together.

Swift, Addison, and Pope, mayhap
They sauntered slowly past her,
Or printer's boy, with gown and cap,
For Steele went trotting faster.

For beau nor wit had she a look,
Nor lord nor lady minding;
She bent her head above this book,
Attentive to her binding.

11.

And one stray thread of golden hair,
Caught on her nimble fingers,
Was stitched within this volume, where
Until to-day it lingers.

Past and forgotten, beaux and fair ;
Wigs, powder, all out-dated ;
A queer antique, the Sedan chair ;
Pope, stiff and antiquated.

Yet as I turn these odd old plays,
This single stray lock finding,
I'm back in those forgotten days,
And watch her at her binding.

MARJORIE'S KISSES.

WALTER LEARNED.

MARJORIE laughs and climbs on my knee,
And I kiss her and she kisses me.
I kiss her, but I don't much care,
Because, although she is charming and fair,
Marjorie's only three.

But there will come a time, I ween,
When, if I tell her of this little scene,
She will smile and prettily blush, and then
I shall long in vain to kiss her again,
When Marjorie's seventeen.

MY MEERSCHAUMS.

CHARLES F. LUMMIS.

LONG pipes and short ones, straight and curved,
   High carved and plain, dark-hued and creamy ;
Slim tubes for cigarettes reserved,
   And stout ones for Havanas dreamy.

This cricket on an amber spear
   Impaled, recalls that golden weather
When love and I, too young to fear
   Heartburn, smoked cigarettes together.

And even now — too old to take
   The little papered shams for flavor —
I light it oft for her sweet sake
   Who gave it, with her girlish favor.

And here's the mighty student bowl
   Whose tutoring in and after college
Has led me nearer Wisdom's goal
   Than all I learned of text-book knowledge.

" It taught me ? " Aye, to hold my tongue,
   To keep a-light and yet burn slowly ;
To break ill spells about me flung
   As with the enchanted whiff of Moly !

This narghileh, whose hue betrays
　　Perique from soft Louisiana,
In Egypt once beguiled the days
　　Of Tewfik's dreamy-eyed Sultana.

Speaking of color, do you know
　　A maid with eyes as darkly splendid
As are the hues that rich and slow
　　On this Hungarian bowl have blended?

Can artist paint the fiery glints
　　Of this quaint finger here beside it,
With amber nail — the lustrous tints,
　　A thousand Partagas have dyed it?

" And this old silver patched affair? "
　　Well, sir, that meerschaum has its reasons
For showing marks of time and wear ;
　　For in its smoke through fifty seasons

My grandsire blew his cares away !
　　And, then, when done with life's sojourning,
At seventy-five dropped dead one day,
　　That pipe between his set teeth burning!

" Killed him? " No doubt ! it's apt to kill
　　In fifty years' incessant using —
Some twenty pipes a day. And still,
　　On that ripe, well filled lifetime musing,

I envy oft so bright a part —
　　To live as long as life's a treasure ;

To die of — not an aching heart,
 But — half a century of pleasure !

Well, well !   I'm boring you, no doubt ;
 How these old memories will undo one —
I see you've let your weed go out —
 That's wrong !   Here, light yourself a new one !

MY CIGARETTE.

CHARLES F. LUMMIS.

MY cigarette! The amulet
   That charms afar unrest and sorrow;
The magic wand that far beyond
   To-day, can conjure up to-morrow.
Like love's desire, thy crown of fire
   So softly with the twilight blending;
And ah! meseems, a poet's dreams
   Are in thy wreaths of smoke ascending.

My cigarette! Can I forget
   How Kate and I, in sunny weather,
Sat in the shade the elm-tree made
   And rolled the fragrant weed together?
I at her side beatified,
   To hold and guide her fingers willing;
She rolling slow the paper's snow,
   Putting my heart in with the filling.

My cigarette! I see her yet,
   The white smoke from her red lips curling,
Her dreaming eyes, her soft replies,
   Her gentle sighs, her laughter purling!

7*   118

Ah, dainty roll, whose parting soul
   Ebbs out in many a snowy billow,
I too would burn if I could earn
   Upon her lips so soft a pillow !

Ah, cigarette ! The gay coquette
   Has long forgot the flames she lighted,
And you and I unthinking by
   Alike are thrown, alike are slighted.
The darkness gathers fast without,
   A rain-drop on my window plashes ;
My cigarette and heart are out,
   And naught is left me but the ashes.

A BOUTONNIÈRE.

JEROME A. HART.

A BOUTONNIÈRE! A dainty thing···
Were I a poet I would sing
In flowing verse thy beauties rare,
    O boutonnière!

The steel-clad knight wore on his crest
A ribbon from his lady's breast;
The modern lover still doth wear
    Her boutonnière.

A bud from her corsage bouquet,
Some heliotrope in volute spray,
A tendril, too, of maiden's-hair —
    Ah, boutonnière,

Those tendrils wind around my heart,
The rose-bud's thorns have made me smart —
Would I could think thou wert no snare,
    O boutonnière!

DECEPTION.

CHARLES HENRY LÜDERS.

IT took just a day to discover
   That all my precautions were *nil*.
I loved her — ah ! how I did love her —
   And, I must confess, love her still.

As we walked where the moon lit the woolly
   White back of each in-coming wave,
She seemed to reciprocate fully
   The tender affection I gave.

We parted. Last week she was married :
   The wedding was private and nice.
On leaving, the couple were harried
   With slippers and handfuls of rice.

And now she is back in the city,
   Installed in the coziest home,
With a husband who thinks it a pity
   An hour from his " precious " to roam.

And *I* —well, I count myself lucky;
   And need no consoling, for she —
The dear little darling, the " ducky " —
   Was good enough to — marry *me*.

AN AMERICAN GIRL.

BRANDER MATTHEWS.

SHE'S had a Vassar education,
   And points with pride to her degrees ;
She's studied household decoration ;
   She knows a dado from a frieze,
   And tells Corots from Boldinis ;
A Jacquemart etching, or a Haden,
   A Whistler, too, perchance might please
A frank and free young Yankee maiden.

She does not care for meditation ;
   Within her bonnet are no bees ;
She has a gentle animation,
   She joins in singing simple glees.
   She tries no trills, no rivalries,
With Lucca (now Baronin Raden)
   With Nilsson or with Gerster ; she's
A frank and free young Yankee maiden.

I'm blessed above the whole creation,
    Far, far, above all other he's,
I ask you for congratulation
    On this the best of jubilees ;
    I go with her across the seas
Unto what Poe would call an Aiden,—
    I hope no serpents there to tease
A frank and free young Yankee maiden.

ENVOY.

Princes, to you the western breeze
    Bears many a ship and heavy laden,
What is the best we send in these ?
    A frank and free young Yankee maiden.

THE BALLADE OF ADAPTATION

BRANDER MATTHEWS.

THE native drama's sick and dying.
   So say the cynic critic crew :
The native dramatist is crying—
    " Bring me the paste ! Bring me the glue !
    Bring me the pen, and scissors, too !
Bring me the works of E. Augier !
    Bring me the works of V. Sardou !
I am the man to write a play.'

For want of plays the stage is sighing,
   Such is the song the wide world through :
The native dramatist is crying—
    " Behold the comedies I brew !
    Behold my dramas not a few !
On German farces I can prey,
    And English novels I can brew ;
/ am the man to write a play ! "

There is, indeed, no one denying
    That fashion's turned from old to new :
The native dramatist is crying--
    "Molière, good-by ! Shakespeare, adieu ! '
I do not think so much of you.
Although not bad, you've had your day,
    And for the present you won't do,
I am the man to write a play ! "

Prince of the stage, don't miss the cue,
    A native dramatist, I say
To every cynic critic, " Pooh !
    I am the man to write a play ! "

MEA CULPA.

EDWARD S. MARTIN.

THERE is a thing which in my brain,
   Though nightly I revolve it,
I cannot in the least explain,
   Nor do I hope to solve it.
While others tread the narrow path
   In manner meek and pious,
Why is it that my spirit hath
   So opposite a bias?

I had no yearnings, when a boy,
   To sport an angel's wrapper;
Nor heard I with tumultuous joy
   The church-frequenting clapper.
My action always harmonized
   With my own sweet volition;
I always did what I devised,
   But rarely asked permission.

I went to school. To study? No!
   I dearly loved to dally,
And dawdle over Ivanhoe,
   Tom Brown, and Charles O'Malley.

In recitation I was used
　To halt on every sentence;
Repenting, seldom I produced
　Fruits proper for repentance.

At college later I became
　Familiar with my Flaccus;
Brought incense to the Muses' flame,
　And sacrificed to Bacchus.
I flourished in an air unfraught
　With sanctity's aroma;
Learned many things I was not taught,
　And captured a diploma.

I am not well provided for,
　I have no great possessions;
I do not like the legal or
　Medicinal professions.
Were I of good repute, I might
　Take orders as a deacon :
But I'm no bright and shining light,
　But just a warning beacon.

Though often urged by friends sincere
　To wed a funded houri,
I cannot read my title clear
　To any damsel's dowry;
And could to wedlock I induce
　An heiress, I should falter,
For fear that such a bridal noose
　Might prove a gilded halter.

My tradesmen have suspicious grown,
   My friends are tired of giving;
Upon the cold, cold world I'm thrown
   To hammer out a living.
I fear that work before me lies;
   Indeed, I see no option,
Unless perhaps I advertise —
   "An orphan for adoption."

INFIRM.

EDWARD S. MARTIN.

" I WILL not go, " he said, " for well
   I know her eyes' insidious spell,
And how unspeakable he feels
Who takes no pleasure in his meals.
I know a one idea man
Should undergo the social ban,
And if she once my purpose melts,
I know I'll think of nothing else."

" I care not though her teeth are pearls —
The town is full of nicer girls ;
I care not though her lips are red —
It does not do to lose one's head ;
I'll give her leisure to discover,
For once, how little I think of her ;
And then, how will she feel ? " cried he,
And took his hat and went to see.

THE ROSE SHE WORE IN WINTER.

LOUISE CHANDLER MOULTON.

O ROSE, so subtly sweet,
   What dost thou in the snow—
The time of frost and sleet,
   When roses should not blow—
   Playing at summer so ?

When we that beauty meet,
   Which nightingales in June
For love and bliss entreat,
   With what cold, wintry rune
   Shall we thy praise entune ?

My Rose, so subtly sweet,
   Thy rose-red lips I kiss ;
I kneel at thy dear feet,
   Dear Rose, and do not miss
   The summer's bygone bliss.

A LITTLE COMEDY.

LOUISE CHANDLER MOULTON.

IS the world the same, do you think, my dear,
　　As when we walked by the sea together,
And the white caps danced and the cliffs rose sheer
　　And we were glad in the autumn weather?

You played at loving that day, my dear—
　　How well you told me that tender story—
And I made answer, with smile and tear,
　　While the sky was flushed with the sunset's glory.

Now I shut my eyes, and I see, my dear,
　　That far-off path by the surging ocean—
I shut my eyes, and I seem to hear
　　Your voice surmounting the tide's commotion.

It was but a comedy slight, my dear—
　　Why should its memory come to vex me?
Can it be I am longing that you should appeal
　　And play it again?　My thoughts perplex me.

'Tis the sea and the shore that I miss, my dear—
  The sea and the shore, and the sunset's glory—
Or would these be nothing without you near,
  To murmur again that fond, old story ?

I know you now but too well, my dear—
  With your heart as light as a wind-blown feather—
Yet somehow the world seems cold and drear
  Without your acting, this autumn weather.

IN WINTER.

LOUISE CHANDLER MOULTON.

O TO go back to the days of June,
  Just to be young and alive again,
Hearken again to the mad, sweet tune
  Birds were singing with might and main :
South they flew at the summer's wane,
  Leaving their nests for storms to harry,
Since time was coming for wind and rain
  Under the wintry skies to marry.

Wearily wander by dale and dune
  Footsteps fettered with clanking chain—
Free they were in the days of June,
  Free they never can be again :
Fetters of age and fetters of pain,
  Joys that fly, and sorrows that tarry—
Youth is over, and hope were vain
  Under the wintry skies to marry.

Now we chant but a desolate rune—
   " O to be young and alive again ! "—
But never December turns to June,
   And length of living is length of pain :
Winds in the nestless trees complain,
   Snows of winter about us tarry,
And never the birds come back again
   Under the wintry skies to marry.

ENVOI.

Youths and maidens, blithesome and vain,
   Time makes thrusts that you cannot parry,
Mate in season, for who is fain
   Under the wintry skies to marry ?

THE BALLADE OF THE ENGAGED
YOUNG MAN.

OH, I am engaged to be married now,
   And fondly dream of the happy day
When orange blossoms shall deck her brow ;
   She's fixed the date for the month of May.
   And yet to myself I softly say,
As her holiday presents go ding-a-ling
   On the jeweler's flashing crystal tray,
" I wish I had put it off till spring ! "

As a prince I am merry, all allow ;
   I'm like a bird in the hawthorn spray,
Or a clam when the tide is high, I vow,
   Or a child with his latest toy at play.
   Yet I have to think, as I coolly lay
My earnings down to hear Patti sing,
   " Though my lady's an angel in every way,
I wish I had put it off till spring ! "
          8*   155

I dance and I romp and I wonder how
 I should ever be happy or blithe or gay,
Did not Love with his sweets my heart endow —
 (He endowed when she said she'd be mine for aye)
 Yet when roses I get, or the bright coupé,
And down to the charity ball we wing,
 I fancy of sense I have not a ray,
And wish I had put it off till spring !

ENVOI.

Young man, I am neither old nor gray ;
 But I can inform you of just one thing :
You'll chant, if you get her December " Yea,"
 " I wish I had put it off till spring ! "

AN OLD BEAU.

R. K. MUNKITTRICK.

FULL often I think in my trim swallow-tail,
At parties where flowers their fragrance exhale,
Of times when my pate was a bower of curls,
And I danced with the grandmas of all the dear girls.

I look on the charms that their beauties unfold —
They seem the same damsels while I have grown old.
I feel like white winter without a warm ray ;
They look like the roses that blossom in May.

But winter may look with its shiver and chill
Through the windows at flowers that bloom on the sill,
And I may ask Edith with ringlets of jet
If she will dance with me the next minuet.

I go to all parties, receptions, first nights,
I'm a merry old bird in my fanciful flights :
I may look, like the winter, a snowy old thing,
But deep in my heart dwells the spirit of spring.

I know that I am not as old as I look,
My voice has no crack and my back has no crook ;
And happy I'd be if May, Maud, and Lucille
Would treat me as one who's as young as I feel.

PRÆSENS REGNAT.

DUFFIELD OSBORNE.

HOW often have I asked thee, dear,
  If thou didst love but me ?
How oft thy whisper in mine ear
  Hath answered tenderly ?

And deftly I the truth can trace
  That in that answer lies.
For I do ever see my face
  Deep pictured in thine eyes.

Ah me ! a tale of broken vows
  Is ringing mournfully,
A bird that dwells among the boughs
  Hath sung a song to me.

Think not he sang her heart to win,
  Trust not her eyes ; beware !
For whosoever looks therein
  Beholds his likeness there !

138

TO A CORKSCREW.

DUFFIELD OSBORNE.

THOU who to burdened brain, and troubled heart
  Dost wind thy way with gently sinuous art,
Slender, and graceful, curled with skill divine :
Mirth, riot, and revelry are ever thine
Whose office 'tis to seek and free the captive wine.

Hail ! to thee men below and gods above
Attune their lays of homage and of love :
Fair silver ringlet ! thou dost ever cling
With truer faith to peasant and to king
Than curls of brown or gold that lovesick poets sing.

WE PARTED AT THE OMNIBUS.

DONN PLATT.

WE parted at the omnibus, I never can forget
    Your eyes, my dove, like stars above, with dew
      were heavy wet ;
Your luggage, love, I handed up as the driver round
    did pull.
I could not speak for, O my heart, like the omnibus,
    was full.

Your slender hand's six-buttoned glove lay nestling soft
    in mine.
Your clinging gown, my sweetest love, in fit was just
    divine ;
" Through life, my pet, I go with thee," I tremblingly
    begun,
When spoke a German passenger, " Dere's only zeats
    vor vun."

My miniature you had, my face all painted smooth and
    bland ;
Your photo, love, you gave me as the agent gave his
    hand ;

14

" You'll write to me, I know you will, this aching
 heart to ease,
And every line from you will be "—" Miss, ten cents,
 if you please."

I put you in a corner, dear, to take that dreary ride,
I saw a suit of stripèd tweed close sitting by your side;
With gun and hound from out the town to hunt 'twas
 going down,
I heard a suit of rusty black call stripes a Mr. Brown.

With wooden damn the stage-door slammed, and shut
 me from your sight,
My heart went throbbing "all is wrong!" the agent
 cried " all right!"
From out my life, you rolled away with unexpected
 speed,
Three trotting hat-racks in the team, a rocker in the
 lead.

The war came on, as volunteer my gallant troops I led,
And lost a leg at Shiloh, when old Sherman lost his
 head ;
And Brown was there, a sutler bold, resplendent in the
 blue,
He fought for flag and country where the profits did
 accrue.

When Peace her downy pinions spread o'er all our land
    and sea,
I stumped me home a veteran with war's sad legacy :
I sought you, love, to find alas ! no footing left to me,
For General Brown was to the front, a millionaire was
    he.

'Twas at a grand re-union giv'n in honor of our cause,
The banners waved, the champagne popped, I got
    some wild applause :
I saw you enter, sweet and fair, the General led you
    down,
You leaned to him so lovingly, he called you **Mrs.
Brown.**

AT MRS. MILLIDOR'S.

SYDNEY HERBERT PIERSON.

I WAS down at the Millidors' Thursday,—
    They receive on that evening, you know,—
And could hardly have chosen a worse day,
    With the slush, and the rain, and the snow;
But the parlors were filled to o'erflowing,—
    Lots of people you know, I presume,—
But I thought it was dull, and was going,
    When Ethel came into the room.

There was Mrs. Fitz-Simmons de Brown there,
    Who gave such a dinner last fall;
And every one else in the town there,
    Who's really worth knowing at all:
Miss Tinsel, considered a Hebe
    By people who know or assume —
You'd have wondered how ever could she be
    When Ethel came into the room.

There was fat Mrs. Space and a lady
    (A widow that never wore weeds)
Hinting somebody's past was too shady:
    Miss Slur, sowing venomous seeds;

Miss Wilted, sarcastic and spiteful,
    Putting Dowager Dash in a fume:
How odd they should be so delightful
    When Ethel came into the room.

Of course there were long recitations,
    Some songs sprinkled in here and there,
Not to mention the minor vexations
    One had to look pleased at and bear;
Spout, primed with those verses from Browning
    He'll recite till the trumpet of doom:
Ah! he was the only one frowning
    When Ethel came into the room.

A girl with a mournful expression
    Was speaking a dolorous thing —
A horrible sort of confession
    Of dead hopes and years taken wing.
She had throttled a passion: 'twas fearful
    How the corpse would stalk out of its tomb;
But it seemed, on the whole, rather cheerful
    When Ethel came into the room.

The dowagers' wrinkled old faces
    Grew older by ten years or more,
The color of costly old laces,
    The rest not a bit as before.
In the air was a sound as the humming
    Of bees, and a subtle perfume
Then I knew ere I looked she was coming,
    When Ethel came into the room.

But there's always a fly in the ointment,
    The lute has a rift, as a rule;
Joy brings in its train disappointment,
    And tears choke the jest of the fool;
So I thought of that swell marriage lately,
    Where gouty old Crœsus was groom,
As he ambled behind her sedately
    When Ethel came into the room.

BALLADE OF MIDSUMMER.

SYDNEY HERBERT PIERSON.

THROUGH murky panes of dusty glass
   Where swarm slow, sleepy flies, I gaze
Down on the street. Like burnished brass
  The stones reflect the sun's hot rays ;
  I hear the heavy-laden drays
Go rumbling through the dust and dirt;
  In thought I see the cliffs and bays
At Newport or at Mount Desert.

At length upon the breeze-swept grass
  I watch the ocean through the haze,
And one besides, whose smiles surpass
  All nature's wiles. The sea-wind plays
  Among her locks. A nymph who strays,
Blue-jerseyed, in a kilted skirt.
  Ah me ! the hearts she snares and slays
At Newport or at Mount Desert.

Time flies no more for me, alas !
    He only comes and idly stays,
Too warm to make the moments pass
    And hurry on vacation's days;
    While tantalizing fancies raise
Cool dreams of beaches ocean-girt,
    Beyond the city's busy maze,
At Newport or at Mount Desert.

ENVOY.

Fate, lead me by those summer ways
    Where happy mortals dance and flirt,
And thou shalt have thy meed of praise
    At Newport or at Mount Desert.

VIOLETS.

ERNEST DE LANCEY PIERSON

VIOLETS, dainty and sweet.
  Born of the dews and the May
Not in the dust and the heat
  I leave you to perish to-day.

Nay, in the lordliest state
  Proud shall you go to your rest
Kings could but envy your fate
  Dying to-night on her breast

168

BLOWING BUBBLES.

ERNEST DE LANCEY PIERSON.

I CAN see you standing there
 In your Watteau dress
By the tapestry portière,
Firelight on your yellow hair,
Daintier I'm sure was ne'er
 Dresden shepherdess.

Laughingly you stooped and blew
 Bubbles in the air :
Globes of irridescent hue,
Flashing opals, bright as dew —
But my eyes were all on you,
 Queenly, standing there.

I, upon that very night,
 Formed a bubble too,
Silvery with your smiles, and bright
With your blue eyes' lustrous light
That seemed ever to invite
 One to come and woo.

169

Frail my argosy, and fair
    With delusive hope ;
Soon, ah ! soon, to my despair,
Learned I when it burst in air
It was made—as others were
    Only out of soap !

AN APRIL MAID.

SAMUEL MINTURN PECK.

TRIPPING through the April breeze
  In a kirtle blue,
Brighter blossom mellow bees
  Ne'er in summer woo.

From her little scarlet mouth
  Rills of song are gliding,
Ballads of the balmy South
  In her memory biding.

She is winsome, she is shy,
  Clad in sweet apparel;
Like the song of Lorelei
  Floats her dainty carol.

Round about her wayward hair
  Tricksy fairies hover,
Tripping sunbeams unaware —
  Who could choose but love her!

Up and down her velvet cheek
  Dimples chase her blushes,
Will she listen if I speak
  When her carol hushes?

Be my fate or drear or bright,
Soon, ah soon, I'll know it;
If I may not be her knight,
Still I'll be her poet.

A SOUTHERN GIRL.

SAMUEL MINTURN PECK.

H ER dimpled cheeks are pale;
   She's a lily of the vale,
      Not a rose.
In a muslin or a lawn
She is fairer than the dawn
      To her beaus.

Her boots are slim and neat,—
She is vain about her feet
      It is said.
She amputates her *r*'s,
But her eyes are like the stars
      Overhead.

On a balcony at night
With a fleece cloud of white
      Round her hair —
Her grace, ah, who could paint ?
She would fascinate a saint,
      I declare.

'Tis a matter of regret,
She's a bit of a coquette
      Whom I sing :

On her cruel path she goes
With a half-a-dozen beaus
    To her string.

But let all of that pass by,
As her maiden moments fly
    Dew empearled;
When she marries, on my life,
She will make the dearest wife
    In the world.

COURTING AN HEIRESS.

WALLACE PECK.

The Lover.

A HUNDRED thousand pens have traced
  The ecstasies of love :
A hundred thousand hearts have graced
  That boon from gods above.
A hundred thousand maids have shared
  In Cupid's fond desire ;
A hundred thousand youths have dared,
  For love, the parents' ire.
A hundred thousand pairs, I ween,
  Will wedded be ere long,
What says my hundred thousand Queen—
  Shall *we* augment the throng ?

The Heiress.

A hundred thousand times I've said,
  " Oh, heart ! your wish I know "
These hundred thousand tears I shed
  Hymeneal longings show

155

A hundred thousand sighs—nor less—
　　I've cast, when we're apart ;
A hundred thousand times now press
　　Me to your loving heart.
I'll send a hundred thousand miles
　　To order my *trousseau*
And we'll to the (hundred) Thousand Isles
　　After the wedding go.

TO A SLIPPER.

WILLIAM THEODORE PETERS.

TO this complexion has your faded satin
　　With much ill usage come at last, and so
You stand in haughty silence on my mantle,
　　A high-heeled slipper with a pointed toe.
Does there still linger in your dainty creases
　　Some faint, dim flutterings of soft regret
For gay young hearts that once beat time so wildly,
　　Watching you tripping through the minuet?

What of sweet faces brave in rouge and patches,
　　And powdered heads and men in smalls arrayed,
Half mad with admiration at your glancing
　　From quilted petticoat and stiff brocade?
What of soft eyes, round arms, and burning blushes?
　　What of the gallant Tory in nankeen
Who made such fine remarks that evening, walking
　　Along the Battery to Bowling Green?

What of the catches trolled, the treasonous ballads,
　　The brilliant wit about the steaming bowl
Of Christmas punch? Ah! surely such bright memories
　　Must still be stored within your leather sole.

And tell me, was not that the gladdest scene, and merriest
  Of all the many scenes you moved among —
The day that Polly Henderson was married in you,
    The slipper only held its satin tongue?

TATTING.

DAVID L. PROUDFIT.

WITH figure demure, and downcast face,
And a tranquil air of quiet grace,
Her delicate fingers deftly wrought
A pattern as fine as a fairy's thought,
Tatting that day !

Oh, maiden fair, with the silken hair,
And the shining eyes of a lustre rare,
What abracadabra, mysterious spell
Is thy flying shuttle weaving so well,
Tatting to-day.

Ah, sir, I work to have my way
In the perfumed air of a gracious day,
My nimble fingers are weaving a snare
To entangle human hearts. Beware
Of my tatting to-day.

So the lily fingers, entrancing flew,
And the lustrous eyes were heavenly blue ;
And the silken hair was shot with gold,
And down in a golden glory rolled,
Tatting that day.

159

And she had her will on a gracious day,
All clad in a cloud of white array ;
And I bless the day and the perfumed air
That kissed her cheek as she wove her snare,
    Tatting that day.

DOWN THE SWITCHBACK

DAVID L. SPOUDFIT.

SIDE by side we rode together,
  On a clear October day,
While the mountains crimson-crested
  Kept a royal holiday.
Down the Switchback from Mount Pisgah
  We went speeding o'er the hills.
With the golden sunlight flashing
  From the rippling mountain rills,
But the flashing and the glinting,
  And the blue of autumn skies.
Were but frosty in their beauty
  To the summer of her eyes.
Side by side we rode together,
  And I did not dare to wait
For she was seventeen, and I
  Was turned of forty-eight.

So I whispered to her, " Darling
  Let us travel, side by side,
Down the grade of Life's long Switchback.
  To the shoreless ocean's tide."

But she looked away far over
  All the hills that lay between,
To the distant, dim horizon,
  And her eyes were *too* serene
As she said, " I like October,
  With its splendors of decay.
But I like the springtime better,
  And the warm, sweet air of May.
Thus we travelled down the Switchback.
  Thus I trifled with my fate :
For she was seventeen, and I
  Was turned of forty-eight.

IF.

JAMES JEFFREY ROCHE.

OH, if the world were mine, Love,
  I'd give the world for thee !
Alas ! there is no sign, Love,
  Of that contingency.

Were I a king,— which isn't
  To be considered now,—
A diadem had glistened
  Upon that lovely brow.

Had fame with laurels crowned me,—
  She hasn't, up to date,—
Nor time nor change had found me
  To love and thee ingrate.

If Death threw down his gage, Love,
  Though life is dear to me,
I'd die, e'en of old age, Love,
  To win a smile from thee.

But being poor, we part, dear,
  And love, sweet love, must die ;
Thou wilt not break thy heart, dear,
  No more, I think, shall I !

DON'T.

JAMES JEFFREY ROCHE.

YOUR eyes were made for laughter;
  Sorrow befits them not;
Would you be blithe hereafter,
  Avoid the lover's lot.

The rose and lily blended
  Possess your cheeks so fair;
Care never was intended
  To leave his furrows there.

Your heart was not created
  To fret itself away,
Being unduly mated
  To common human clay.

But hearts were made for loving —
  Confound philosophy!
Forget what I've been proving,
  Sweet Phyllis, and love me!

COQUETTE.

HARRISON ROBERTSON.

"COQUETTE," my love they sometimes call,
   For she is light of lips and heart:
What though she smile alike on all,
   If in her smiles she knows no art?

Like some glad brook she seemes to be,
   That ripples o'er its pebbly bed,
And prattles to each flower or tree,
   Which stoops to kiss it, overhead.

Beneath the heavens white and blue
   It purls and sings and laughs and leaps,
The sunny meadows dancing through
   O'er noisy shoals and frothy steeps.

'Tis thus the world doth see the brook;
   But I have seen it otherwise
When following it to some far nook
   Where leafy shields shut out the skies.

And there its waters rest, subdued,
   In shadowy pools, serene and shy,
Wherein grave thoughts and fancies brood,
   And tender dreams and longings lie.

I love it when it laughs and leaps,
　But love is better when at rest —
'Tis only in its tranquil deeps
　I see my image in its breast!

TWO TRIOLETS.

HARRISON ROBERTSON.

What he said.

THIS kiss upon your fan I press —
　　Ah! Sainte Nitouche, you don't refuse it!
And may it from its soft recess —
This kiss upon your fan I press —
Be blown to you, a shy caress,
　　By this white down, whene'er you use it.
This kiss upon your fan I press,—
　　Ah, Sainte Nitouche, you *don't* refuse it!

What she thought.

　　To kiss a fan!
　　　　What a poky poet!
　　The stupid man
　　To kiss a fan
　　When he knows — that — he — can —
　　　　Or ought to know it —
　　To kiss a fan!
　　　　What a poky poet!

187

APPROPRIATION.

HARRISON ROBERTSON.

ONE day, one balmy "day of days,'
　　I fortunately found her
Down in the sweet old garden's maze,
　　Hid by its bloom around her.
She stood beneath the apple-tree,
　　Against it idly leaning,
Gazing with eyes that did not see,
　　A-dream with subtle meaning.

She stood in snowy stuff bedight,
　　Her lips a rose caressing,
Against the tree one nude and white
　　Round arm her cheek was pressing.
Rich-favored tree — its boughs above
　　In flaky banks were blowing,
Which, at the nearness of my love,
　　In tender pink were glowing.

I paused, yet loth to spoil the scene,
　　Content to thus adore her ;
And then the shrubbery between
　　I made my way before her.

A start — the slightest did it seem
　　To me — such was my greeting.
Ah! had I been part of that dream
　　Which scarcely yet was fleeting?

" I come into your life, my dear,
　　As in your dream," I told her.
" I love you, and your place is here "—
　　" Here " being next my shoulder.
Her place was there, her face was there
　　Within her hands all hidden;
And on her rippling, sunny hair
　　I pressed a kiss unchidden.

How sweet, among the apple-trees,
　　The silent spell that bound us,
With naught but languid bloom and bees
　　And mating birds around us!
" You have not said you love me yet,"
　　At last I whispered to her.
She raised her eyes — ah! were they wet?—
　　And as I nearer drew her,

Within their tender depths I read
　　The answer I'd entreated;
No words of lips could have unsaid
　　What those soft eyes repeated.
And then, with coy, maternal air,
　　She smiled and touched my forehead,
" And, Jack, you must not comb your hair
　　So high," she said —" it's horrid! "

THE RHYME OF A FAN.

LIZETTE WOODWORTH REESE.

PAINT Anastasia as a saint :
  Priscilla as a Puritan,
Holding long lily-stalks , but paint
  Dear Dolly with a fan !

It is a page wherefrom we read
  Each word she has to say ;
Learn who may come, and who must speed,
  And who may near her stay.

It is a wall as stout as stone,
  Where sweet and cold of face,
When 'tis her mood she sits alone
  Behind its frill of lace.

'Tis covered thick with blossoms small
  Red-tinted like the morn ;
And he who'd dare to scale that wall
  Would find each rose a thorn.

Ah, Dolly, Dolly ! we confess,
  Amongst us all there's not a man,
But knows he's loved a *little less*
  Than your quaint silken fan !

A ROSEBUD.

THE sad South lurks about her mouth,
   The North is in her eyes ;
She is the bough with bloom of snow—
The sweetest weather that we know—
   She is both warm and wise.

The sad South taught those tricks of fan,
   Those dainty, Old World ways ;
And watching her, we seem to be
In Spain ; gray streets slip to the sea,
   And roofs are dim with haze.

But, ah ! her eyes are Saxon blue !
   So we must watch again ;
Straightway the tall thorn hedges blow,
The nightingales sing loud, sing low,
   Down some dusk Devon lane.

The secret's out.   If South and North
   Be both at Maude's command,
Is it great wonder she's so sweet,
And sends us poor lads to her feet
   With one touch of her hand ?

CLOE TO CLARA.

(*A Saratoga Letter.*)

JOHN G. SAXE.

DEAR CLARA :—I wish you were here:
 The prettiest spot upon earth !
With everything charming, my dear—
 Beaux, badinage, music and mirth !
Such rows of magnificent trees.
 Overhanging such beautiful walks.
Where lovers may stroll, if they please.
 And indulge in the sweetest of talks !

And then, what a gossiping sight !
 What talk about William and Harry :
How Julia was spending last night ;
 And *why* Miss Morton should marry :
Dear Clara, I've happened to see
 Full many a tea-table slaughter.
But, really, scandal with tea
 Is nothing to scandal with water !

'Tis pleasant to guess at the reason—
 The genuine motive which brings
Such all-sorts of folks in the season
 To stop a few days at the Springs.
Some come to partake of the waters,
 The sensible, old-fashioned elves,

Some come to dispose of their daughters,
  And some to dispose of—themselves !

Some come to exhibit their faces
  To new and admiring beholders ;
Some come to exhibit their graces,
  And some to exhibit their shoulders ;
Some come to make people stare
  At the elegant dresses they've got ;
Some to show what a lady may wear,
  And some—what a lady may not !

Some come to squander their treasure,
  And some their funds to improve ;
And some for a mere love of pleasure.
  And some for the pleasure of love ;
And some to escape from the old,
  And some to see what is new ;
But most—it is plain to be told—
  Come here—because other folks do !

And that, I suppose, is the reason
  Why *I* am enjoying to-day
What's called " the height—of the season "
  In rather the loftiest way.
Good-by—for now I must stop—
  To Charley's command I resign—
So I'm his for the regular hop,
  But ever most tenderly thine.

A REASONABLE PETITION.

JOHN G. SAXE.

YOU say, dearest girl, you esteem me,
  And hint of respectful regard,
And I'm certain it wouldn't beseem me
  Such an excellent gift to discard.

But even the Graces, you'll own,
  Would lose half their beauty apart —
And Esteem, when she stands all alone,
  Looks most unbecomingly tart.

So grant me, dear girl, this petition :—
  If Esteem ere again should come hither,
Just to keep her in cheerful condition,
  Let Love come in company with her '

TO A CHINESE IDOL.

CLINTON SCOLLARD.

O NCE you ruled, a god divine,
  In a sacred shady shrine,
Near a river dark as wine,
      'Mid the trees ;
And to you the mandarins,
With their smooth unshaven chins,
Prayed absolvence from their sins
      On their knees.

Tiny-footed Chinese maids,
With their raven hair in braids,
Sought you in your quiet shades
      'Neath the boughs ;
Haply for a thousand years
You beheld their smiles and tears,
Listened to their hopes and fears
      And their vows.

Now above her escritoire
In my lady's pink boudoir,
Ever dumbly pining for
      Lost repose,

You sit stolid, day by day,
With your cheeks so thin and gray,
Stony eyes and *retroussé*
       Little nose.

Where the sunlight glinteth o'er
Persian rug and polished floor,
You will frown forevermore,
       Grim as hate;
A divinity cast down,
Having neither shrine nor crown,
Once a god, but now a brown
       Paper-weight!

AT THE LETTER-BOX.

CLINTON SCOLLARD.

CLAD in the gem of frocks,
    By the green letter-box,
With her short wavy locks
        Bound by no fetter,

Musing I see her stand,
Raise her arm slowly, and
Drop from a slender hand
        One little letter.

I can't acquaintance claim,
Know not her tender name,
Yet will my fancy frame
        Romances of her.

That the neat *billet-doux*,
Perfumed — of creamy hue,
So lately lost to view
        Is to her lover.

Somehow I seem to feel
That he made strong appeal,
Said he'd be "true as steel,"
        Ever her "Harry";

But that she bade him wait,
Called him precipitate,
Hinted her happy fate —
            Never to marry.

This is her answer.   This,
Weighted with woe or bliss
(Much in parenthesis
            Many lines under),

Borne from its dark recess,
Soon will its all confess ;
Will it be " no," or " yes ? "—
            Which one, I wonder ?

ROSE LEAVES.

CLINTON SCOLLARD.

WITHIN this fragile urn by chance
    I found them, void of scent and faded,
Reminders of a sweet romance
    That budded, bloomed, and died as they did.

The years have flown in swallow flight
    Since last we met, and I incensed her;
Her eyes have lost their laughing light,
    And Time has long conspired against her.

Here let them lie — the once admired —
    A food for idle contemplation,
Dead as the passion they inspired,
    The ashes of an old flirtation.

AT THE CHURCH DOOR.

HENRY B. SMITH.

A LICE has gone to confession.
   What has the girl to confess?
What little idle transgression
   Causes my sweetheart distress?
   Is it her fondness for dress
That needs a priest's intercession,
And brings that pensive expression
   Into her eyes' loveliness?
   What has the maid to confess?

Is it some little flirtation,
   Ending perhaps in a kiss?
Mine be the sin's expiation,
   If I but shared in its bliss.
   Is it a trifle like this,
Seeking its justification?
Was it a rash exclamation
   Some one has taken amiss?
   Was it a trifle like this?

She who lives always so purely
   Cannot so gravely transgress.
One who can smile so demurely
   Cannot have much to confess.

Let me for pardon address,
For I am guiltier, surely.
Sin your small sins, then, securely;
  If it is I that they bless,
  Mine be the task to confess.

MY MAUSOLEUM.

HENRY B. SMITH.

IT is a crypt, this cabinet ;
  A love affair is buried here ;
Its requiem a faint regret,
  And scented letters for a bier.
Its wreaths, dead roses interlaced
  With memories of ball and *fête*,
While for a headstone I have placed
  A portrait in a paper-weight.

Here lie, as ashes in an urn,
  A verse or two I learned to quote,
The notes I had no heart to burn,
  Our letters,— what a lot we wrote ! —
A silken tress of sunny strands,
  A ribbon that I used to prize,
A glove,— she had such tiny hands,—
  A miniature with deep, dark eyes.

'Tis with a smile I view to-day
  The relics in this cabinet.
When Love is dead and laid away
  We mourn a little, then forget.
The verses quite have left my mind.
  Her rose, her glove, her pictured eyes,
Her letters, are to dust consigned ,
  Their fitting epitaph, " Here — *lies*."

A MARRIAGE À LA MODE.

HENRY B. SMITH.

H AVE you heard what they are saying
    O'er the walnuts and the wine,
Secrets eagerly betraying
    About your affairs and mine?
Foes and friends receive attention
    From each chatting beau and belle,
And they casually mention
    That Marie has "married well."

" Married well!" Ah, that's expressive,
    And from it we understand
That the bridegroom has excessive
    Stores of ducats at command.
Is he good? He has his vices!
    Has he brains? We scarce can tell.
Handsome? Hardly! It suffices,
    If Marie has married well.

Does she love him? Love's a passion,
    Childish in this latter day.
She will dress in height of fashion,
    And her bills he'll promptly pay.
Does he love her? Wildly, madly!
    Since he bought his trotter "Nell,"
He has welcomed naught as gladly;
    Yes, Marie has married well.

Is she happy ?   That's a trifle ;
  Happiness is bought and sold ;
And she readily can stifle
  Love she used to know of old.
Well she knows a heart is broken ;
  As for her's — she cannot tell ;
But her bridal vows are spoken,
  And Marie has married well.

In this game one should give heeding
  To the stakes, not gentle arts ;
And, when diamonds are leading,
  Where's the use of playing hearts ?
I congratulate her gladly ;
  But the wish I can't dispel
That most girls may marry badly,
  If Marie has married well.

AT BAR HARBOR.

S. DECATUR SMITH.

THEY accuse me of flirting with Harry,
    Who hasn't a cent to his name,
And certainly don't mean to marry;
    Such slander's a sin and a shame.

They say I've been often seen walking
    With Harry alone on the rocks;
We've been seen on the sand sitting talking,
    Regardless of custom — and frocks.

They say we were walking together
    The day of that trip to the lake;
And our losing our way in the heather,
    They're certain was *not* a mistake.

At Rodick's, they frequently mention,
    When laughter is noisy and loud,
We, with care to attract no attention,
    Slip quietly off from the crowd.

One nasty old tabby's reported
    She *saw* him one evening last week
(Good gracious! how truth is distorted!)
    Press a kiss on my too-willing cheek.

Such stories as these are invention ;
 The truth in them simply is *nil.*
If I have done the things that they mention,
 It *wasn't* with Harry — 'twas Will!

A WOMAN'S WEAPONS.

S. DECATUR SMITH.

THERE'S a smile, and a glance, and a blush, and a sigh,
　And perhaps, on occasion, a tear ;
There's a delicate touch of a hand, on the sly,
　And a flower she may wear when *he's* near ;

There's a note in her voice that but one may awake,
　And a gleam in her blue (or brown) eye ;
There's a kiss on her lip that *some* fellow may take
　(Now why the deuce isn't it I ?) ;

There's the turn of an ankle, the size of a waist,
　And the way that she does up her hair ;
There's the fit of a glove, and, according to taste,
　The tint of the dress she may wear ;

There are words that are often but semi-expressed,
　And some are hid others below ;
For instance, a " yes " may be frequently guessed
　Through a clearly reversible " no."

Yet her infinite change is her strongest of arms,
　As the song says, "*Femme souvent varie ;*"
But what does she want with such numberless charms,
　When *one* of them finishes me ?

11*　　　　187

AN OLD GLOVE.

DE WITT STERRY.

FOND girl, these tiny slips of kid
  Once your dear, dimpled digits hid,
      And to your elbow pretty
They climbed without the least alarm ;
Or was it that they thought your arm
      The fairest in the city ?

One finger's gone — the middle right :
I use it, dear, when I indite
      My rhymes by yellow tapers,
To shield my finger-nail from ink ;
How would you fare if you — just think ! —
      Lived on the comic papers ?

That night ! Can I forget that night ?
Again I see the candlelight,
      And hear the rippling laughter ;
How many plates I passed between
The openings in that teakwood screen !
      How soon I followed after !

I knew you feigned that stern surprise,
I knew it by your twinkling eyes ;
      Besides, you know your chatter

Fell on a fascinated ear
That time I bent my lips — my dear,
    I'll never breathe the matter.

But I've grown careless of my loves,
And am as bad at crossing gloves
    As turning off a sonnet.
The sight of it just made me grow
A trifle warm, my dear, and so
    I penned these verses on it.

BALLADE OF BARRISTERS.

(Irregular.)

C. C. STARKWEATHER.

TO the shy, sweet face that I saw this morning,
  I toss this kiss from my window-sill,
And mayhap my partner will give me warning
  If I shove not quicker my gray goose-quill.
  I've twenty folios yet to fill.
So it's Blue Eyes, Down! till this deed is drawn;
For Maiden Lane's not a lover's lawn,
  And the rattle of Broadway never is still.

From seal and parchment and dust-covered papers,
  My thoughts fly back to her — *willy nil.*
I lunch at Cable's on lamb and capers,
  And a secret bumper I drain with Phil,
  And I smile when he leaves me to pay the bill.
Oh, it's Blue Eyes, Down! till this deed is drawn;
For Maiden Lane's not a lover's lawn,
  And the rattle of Broadway never is still.

1

My office is no conservatory;
  Its walls are like blanks for a clerk to fill;
But that mignonette, jasmine, and morning-glory
  The charms of a whole hot-house would kill —
  In the white vase there, on the window-sill.
But it's Blue Eyes, Down! till this deed is drawn;
For Maiden Lane's not a lover's lawn,
  And the rattle of Broadway never is still.

ENVOY.

Barristers! with brief-bags to fill,
  It's Blue Eyes, Down! till the deeds are drawn;
  For Maiden Lane's not a lover's lawn,
And the rattle of Broadway never is still.

11

RIVALS.

C. C. STARKWEATHER.

JENNY, how many songs you've chased away!
  To love, I own, is better far than singing.
A host of rhymes surrendered, dear, to-day,
  Or perished in a peal of laughter ringing.

For how am I, by any dreamt-of means,
  To write an Ode to Progress while you're smiling?
Or tell of orange-groves, or dreamy scenes
  Of distant climes, with your sweet voice beguiling?

I've seen the Attic marbles' tinted grace,
  And swung in hammocks 'neath a palace rafter,
But can I match a temple with your face,
  Or weep for Pan before your mocking laughter?

If Pan is dead, you're very much alive!
  And my rapt flights you are forever stopping!
I must be wary if I'd fill my hive,
  And woo the Muse when you have gone out shopping!

PROVENÇAL LOVERS.

(Aucassin and Nicollette.)

EDMUND CLARENCE STEDMAN.

WITHIN the garden of Beaucaire
He met her by a secret stair ;—
The night was centuries ago,
Said Aucassin, " My love, my pet,
These old confessors vex me so !
They threaten all the pains of hell
Unless I give you up, *ma belle* ; "—
Said Aucassin to Nicollette.

" Now who should there in Heaven be
To fill your place, *ma très douce mie* ?
To reach that spot I little care !
There all the droning priests are met ;
All the old cripples, too are there
That unto shrines and altars cling
To filch the Peter-pence we bring ; "—
Said Aucassin to Nicollette.

" There are the barefoot monks and friars
With gowns well-tattered by the briers,
The saints who lift their eyes and whine :
I like them not—a starveling set !
Who'd care with folks like these to dine ?

The other road 'twere just as well
That you and I should take, ma belle !
Said Aucassin to Nicolette.

"To Purgatory I would go
With pleasant comrades whom we know,
Fair scholars, minstrels, lusty Knights
Whose deeds the land will not forget,
The captains of a hundred fights,
True men of valor and degree :
Will join that gallant company,"—
Said Aucassin to Nicollette.

"There, too, are guests and joyance rare,
And beauteous ladies debonair,
The pretty dames, the merry brides
Who with their wedded lords coquette
And have a friend or two besides—
And all in gold and trappings gay,
With furs, and crests in vair and gray : "—
Said Aucassin to Nicollete.

"Sweet players on the cithern strings
And they who roam the world like kings
Are gathered there so blithe and free !
Pardie ! I'd join them now, my pet,
If you went also, *ma douce mie !*
The joys of heaven I'd forego
To have you with me there below,"—
Said Aucassin to Nicollette.

TOUJOURS AMOUR.

EDMUND CLARENCE STEDMAN.

PRITHEE tell me, Dimple-Chin
  At what age does Love begin ?
Your blue eyes have scarcely seen
Summers three, my fairy queen :
But a miracle of sweets,
Soft approaches, sly retreats,
Show the little Archer there,
Hidden in your pretty hair ;
When did'st learn a heart to win ?
Prithee tell me, Dimple-Chin !

" Oh ! " the rosy lips reply.
  " I can't tell you if I try.
'Tis so long I can't remember :
  Ask some younger lass than I ! "

Tell, O tell me, Grizzled-Face
Do your heart and head keep pace ?
When does hoary Love expire,
When do frosts put out the fire ?
Can its embers burn below

All that chill December snow ?
Care you still soft hands to press,
Bonny heads to smoothe and bless ?
When does Love give up the chase ?
Tell, O tell me, Grizzled-Face !

" Ah ! " the wise old lips reply,
   "Youth may pass and strength may die ;
But of Love I can't foretoken :
   Ask some older sage than I ! "

PAN IN WALL STREET

EDMUND CLARENCE STEDMAN.

J UST where the Treasury's marble front
   Looks over Wall Street's mingled nations ;
Where Jews and Gentiles most are wont
   To throng for trade and last quotations :
Where, nour by hour, the rates of gold
   Outrival, in the ears of people,
The quarter chimes, serenely tolled
   From Trinity's undaunted steeple,—

Even here I heard a strange, wild strain
   Sound high above the modern clamor.
Above the cries of greed and gain,
   The curbstone war, the auction's hammer ;
And swift on Music's misty ways,
   It led, from all this strife of millions,
To ancient, sweet-do-nothing days
   Among the kirtle-robed Sicilians.

And as it stilled the multitude,
   And yet more joyous rose, and shriller,
I saw the minstrel where he stood
   At ease against a Doric pillar :

17

One hand a droning organ played,
    The other held a Pan's-pipe (fashioned
Like those of old) to lips that made
    The reeds give out that strain impassioned.

  'Twas Pan himself had wandered here
    A-strolling through this sordid city.
And piping to the civic ear
    The prelude of some pastoral ditty !
The demi-god had crossed the seas—
    From haunts of shepherd, nymph, and satyr,
And Syracusan times--to these
    Far shores and twenty centuries later.

A ragged cap was on his head :
    But—hidden thus—there was no doubting
That, all with crispy locks o'erspread,
    His gnarlèd horns were somewhere sprouting ;
His club-feet, cased in rusty shoes,
    Were crossed, as on some frieze you see them,
And trousers, patched of divers hues,
    Concealed his crooked shanks beneath them.

He filled the quivering reeds with sound,
    And o'er his mouth their changes shifted,
And with his goat's eyes looked around
    Where'er the passing current drifted :
And soon, as on Trinacrian hills
    The nymphs and herdsmen ran to hear him,
Even now the tradesmen from their tills,
    With clerks and porters, crowded near him.

The bulls and bears together drew
 From Jauncey Court and New Street Alley,
As erst, if pastorals be true,
 Came beasts from every wooded valley :
The random passers stayed to list—
 A boxer Ægon, rough and merry,
A Broadway Daphnis, on his tryst
 With Nais at the Brooklyn ferry.

A one-eyed Cyclops halted long
 In tattered cloak of army pattern,
And Galatea joined the throng,—
 A blowzy, apple-vending slattern ;
While old Silenus staggered out
 From some new-fangled lunch-house handy,
And bade the piper, with a shout,
 To strike up Yankee Doodle Dandy !

A newsboy and a peanut girl
 Like little Fauns began to caper ;
His hair was all in tangled curl,
 Her tawny legs were bare and taper :
And still the gathering larger grew,
 And gave its pence and crowded nigher,
While aye the shepherd-minstrel blew
 His pipe, and struck the gamut higher.

O heart of Nature, beating still
 With throbs her vernal passion taught her

Even here, as on the vine-clad hill,
　Or by the Arethusan water !
New forms may fold the speech, new lands
　Arise within these ocean-portals
But Music waves eternal wands,—
　Enchantress of the souls of mortals !

So thought I—but among us trod
　A man in blue, with legal baton,
And scoffed the vagrant demi-god,
　And pushed him from the step I sat on.
Doubting I mused upon the cry,
　" Great Pan is dead ! "—and all the people
Went on their ways :—and clear and high
　The quarter sounded from the steeple.

FRENCH WITH A MASTER.

THEODORE TILTON.

TEACH you French ?   I will, my dear !
  Sit and con your lesson here,
What did Adam say to Eve ?
Aimer, aimer ; c'est à vivre.

Don't pronounce the last word long ;
Make it short to suit the song ;
Rhyme it to your flowing sleeve,
Aimer, aimer ; c'est à vivre.

Sleeve I said, but what's the harm
If I really meant your arm ?
Mine shall twine it by your leave,
Aimer, aimer ; c'est à vivre.

Learning French is full of slips :
Do as I do with the lips :
Here's the right way, you perceive,
Aimer, aimer ; c'est à vivre.

French is always spoken best
Breathing deeply from the chest ;
Darling, does your bosom heave ?
Aimer, aimer ; c'est à vivre.

Now, my dainty little sprite,
Have I taught your lesson right ?
Then what pay shall I receive ?
Aimer, aimer ; c'est à vivre.

Will you think me overbold
If I linger to be told
Whether you yourself believe
Aimer, aimer ; c'est à vivre !

Pretty pupil, when you say
All this French to me to-day,
Do you mean it, or deceive ?
Aimer, aimer ; c'est à vivre.

Tell me, may I understand,
When I press your little hand,
That our hearts together cleave ?
Aimer, aimer ; c'est à vivre.

Have you in your tresses room
For some orange buds to bloom.
May I such a garland weave ?
Aimer, aimer ; c'est à vivre.

Or, if I presume too much,
Teaching French by sense of touch,
Grant me pardon and reprieve !
Aimer, aimer ; c'est à vivre.

Sweetheart, no ! you cannot go !
Let me sit and hold you so ;
Adam did the same by Eve—
Aimer, aimer ; c'est à vivre.

LE GRENIER—American Version.

" *Dans un grenier qu'on est bien à vingt ans.*"
                                        BÉRANGER.

ROBERTSON TROWBRIDGE.

HERE is the street—the house is standing yet '
  Four stories up the little window gleams.
The basement still announces " Rooms to Let ; "
  Through the wide door the dusty sunlight streams.
But how the place has changed !   Across the way
  A tenement its swarming bulk uprears—
'Twas here I weathered it for many a day,
  With Youth and Hope for friends, at Twenty Years.

A small hall-room !   I seek it half by stealth—
  Who cares ? the world may know it if it will !
The worst is told.   I had stout heart, good health,
  A modest clerkship, wants more modest still ;
Companions, too (I had companions then !)—
  What room in all my " up-town palace " hears
Such peals of mirth as yonder little den
  When I and Youth kept house, at Twenty Years !

204

'Twas here I brought my bride.   In that dim place
    The too brief summer of our joy first smiled.
Which of your carpet-knights, my queenly Grace,
    To such a lot will woo your mother's child ?
Just powers ! how dared we to be gay and glad,
    To face the world, unvexed by cramping fears ?
Rash ?—reckless ?   We were mad !—how nobly mad
    With the brave wine of Love and Twenty Years !

Once, as we listened at the window there,
    In the warm sunlight of an April day,
A sound of loyal thunder filled the air—
    The Massachusetts Sixth marched down Broadway.
O gallant hearts and times !   O drum and fife !
    In '62 I joined the volunteers.
Poor wounded soldier, lonely waiting wife,
    We learned what glory meant, at Twenty Years !

It's time to go.   The place looks chill and drear.
    Fate ! were it lot of mine to overlive
But half the happy days I've counted here,
    I'd give—what have I that I would not give ?—
Again to struggle on, to breast the tide,
    To know the worst of Fortune's frowns and fleers,
Brave heart within, my darling by my side,
    And all the world to win, at Twenty Years !

UNDERSTOOD

EDITH SESSIONS TUPPER.

He Speaks.

PAINTED and perfumed, feathered and pink,
  Here is your ladyship's fan.
You gave it to me to hold, I think,
  While you danced with another man.

Downy and soft like your fluffy hair,
  Pink like your delicate face,
The perfume you carry everywhere
  Wafted from feathers and lace.

He Thinks.

Painted and perfumed, dainty and pink,
  A toy to be handled with care ;
It is like your ladyship's self I think,
  A trifle light as air.

For you are a wonderful triumph of art,
  Like a Dresden statuette ;
But you cannot make havoc in my poor heart,
  You innocent-faced coquette.

For I understand those enticing ways
  You practice on every man :
You are only a bit of paint and lace
  Like that delicate toy—your fan.

TO A JAPANESE BABY.

HENRY TYRRELL.

YOU dwell in a dove-cote, where tinkle
  The ornaments hung from the eaves,
Strange trees shade it; blossoms besprinkle
  The dark plumy leaves.

Tea-garden and temple and fountain,
  From out the wide window you view;
And yonder, the snow-crested mountain
  High up in the blue.

On bending your baby eyes nearer,
  Where slumbers the still-watered moat,
You watch, like rose leaves on a mirror,
  The lotos blooms float.

Your face is as brown as a berry,
  In outline as round as a rose;
Black slits of eyes, wakefully merry,
  Slant down to your nose.

Your head, like a friar's, is shaven —
  How droll! not a hair can one find,
Except the tuft, black as a raven,
  That's twisted behind.

Around your form airily flutter
    Fantastic and bright-colored " things ";
You look like a gorgeous, rare butter-
    Fly, resting its wings.

You've soft mats to romp on and tumble ;
    Of furniture, though, there's not much ;
No breakage, to make grown folks grumble —
    No caution, " Don't touch ! "

Your world is so simple and sunny,
    So pleasing and quaint to the eye —
No wonder your plump face grows funny,
    But never can cry.

We love you, Babe Bric-à-brac, dearly,
    Though ne'er have we been to Japan ;
We know your wee dimpled face — merely
    Through this painted fan.

MITTENS.

HENRY TYRRELL.

P URE frost winds, on the winter's eve,
   You play among my lady's tresses,
And pink as apple-bloom you leave
   The cheeks that take your light caresses ;
But from her little hands begone !
   By you they'll not be kissed nor bitten,
For over each is snugly drawn —
   A tiny pale-blue mitten.

The slender, perfume-haunted glove,
   Erstwhile that hid her lily fingers,
Is not the shield that most they love,
   Whereon a pressure honest lingers.
More shy, confiding, tender, true,
   And softer than two curled-up kittens,
Are those dear dainty twins of blue,
   My lady's little mittens.

Once at the play, when lights were low,
   And down had dropped the great green curtain,
I took her hand ; we turned to go ;
   Her fingers clasped o'er mine, I'm certain.

That sudden thrill I feel again,
  That never could be told or written,
Whene'er I see or touch, as then,
  Her downy little mitten.

Some memories those mittens hold,
  And secrets, might one coax confession,
Ah, dearer than a gage of gold
  I'd count if I could gain possession ;
Yet ask her I shall never dare,
  Nor tell her how my heart is smitten,
For fear, in answer to my prayer,
  She might " give me the mitten."

MIS-MATCHED.

HENRY TYRRELL.

O NCE —'twas years ago — I found me
   Moved by magic strange ;
All accustomed earth around me,
   Dreamlike, felt the change.
Berthe was fair.   I learned to love her
   As a flower might do —
For a moment's fondness of her
   Fain had withered, too,
Such love, love does not discover ;
   And she never knew.
Though to none could she be dearer,
Though my heart was far sincerer
   Than the hearts of men,
What could come of all this loving ?
   I was only ten.

Other eyes, full-orbed and tender,
   Drop their curtains fine
With a timid half surrender,
   Now, at glance of mine.

211

Praise, that elsewhere I seek vainly,
    Tempts a soft reply,
Or she says, " I like you," plainly ;
    Edith is not shy.
I but jest and laugh inanely,
    Or repress a sigh.
Yes, I throw away the treasure
(Not without a sense of pleasure,
    And a touch of pain).
What can come of all this loving ?
    She is only ten.

"THE MORNING AFTER."

HAROLD VAN SANTVOORD.

I HEARD a rustle in the hall,
  Where erst we stood 'mid waning tapers ;
She met me in her breakfast-shawl,
  Her crimps all twisted in curl-papers ;
The night before she looked a queen
  In satin sheen and fluffy laces,
But now just where the rouge had been
  Her powder-puff had left its traces.

Beneath the blazing chandelier
  I felt so shy and she so wary,
My brain reeled with a sudden fear
  That she might prove a lissome fairy
And vanish in a golden dream,
  On gauzy wings, if zephyrs wooed her,
Away from aught that she might deem
  The hateful bane of gross intruder.

Alas! a tantalizing shade,
  A cheat, she was, a vain delusion!
Is beauty ever thus to fade ?
  My mind has reached this sad conclusion.
" Oh, face of nature, always true,"
  The poet sang who never chaffed her ;
But, lovely women, ye are few
  Whose faces lure " the morning after."

HER FIRST TRAIN

A. E. WATROUS.

MUSES and Graces appear!
  Fountain Pierian flow!
Greuze in the spirit be near!
  Aid me, O shade of Watteau!
Ancients and moderns a-row,
  Strike me your worthiest strain.
Little my theme do I know —
  'Tis the young lady's First Train.

Ah! in my heart there is fear,
  Chill in its coming as snow;
She who approacheth me here,
  Stately and sweeping and slow —
Could I have romped with her? No
  This duchess? oh, dream most profane!
All that was decades ago —
  'Tis the young lady's First Train.

214

How shall I suit her? It's clear
   Battledore, racquet, and bow
Barred are and banned. In this sphere,
   Certes, I'm somewhat *de trop;*
Still, we accustomed may grow,
   Standing-ground common regain,
Even if — presage of woe! —
   'Tis the young lady's First Train.

L'ENVOI.

Comrades, to friend and to foe
   Thus my changed bearing explain.
Say : " If aught's turned him a beau,
   'Tis the young lady's First Train."

OLD BOHEMIANS.

A. E. WATROUS.

EHEU fugaces! where are they?
　The creeping day, the flying night,
　　The warmth, the color, clamor, light —
Friend of the scythe and hour-glass say
Eheu fugaces! where are they?

Eheu fugaces! where are they?
　　The songs we sang, the cups we quaffed,
　　The eyes that shone, the lips that laughed —
Old mower, went they by your way?
Eheu fugaces! where are they?

Eheu fugaces! where are they?
　　The lights that lined the lonely street,
　　When homeward tripped the dainty feet
That fled against the glance of day —
Eheu fugaces! where are they?

Eheu fugaces! where are they
　　Who walked the ward, who trod the court?
　　Stout fellows all for toil or sport;
Ah, who shall break then he shall pay —
Eheu fugaces! where are they?

Eheu fugaces ! where are they ?
  The old jaw drops, the old veins freeze;
  And where is Lil and where's Louise,
Whose kisses made a "yes " of " nay "—
Eheu fugaces ! where are they ?

Eheu fugaces ! where are they ?
  We've made our running, tossed our dice,
  And Time's are loaded.   In a trice—
Perhaps a year, perhaps a day —
They'll ask : " The garrulous and gray,
Eheu fugaces ! where are they ? "

HER NAME WAS FELICE.

CHARLES HENRY WEBB.

WHEN soft and sweet the summer moon
  Smiled down, and all was peace.
And every pulse of mine kept tune,
  I learned her name—Felice.

First on the beach, then in the brine,
  (Some thought it was my niece)
She laid her little hand in mine,
  And said she was—Felice.

And all who sat along the shore
  And watched the tide's increase,
Knew I was Felix, o'er and o'er,
  Did they think her—Felice?

Still swings on high the self-same moon,
  Still all around seems peace,
Still sit I on the sandy dune,
  But where is she—Felice?

The summer moon still swings on high —
  Oh, summer, must you cease?
Infelicissimus am I?
  But she is still—Felice.

DISCARDED.

CHARLES HENRY WEBB

L AST night I lay on her breast :
  To-day I lie at her feet ;
Then to her heart I was pressed ;
  Now you tread on me, sweet !

Ah, lightly as possible pray—
  Grace for your rose of last night !
If perhaps I look faded to-day,
  Are you quite so fresh in this light ?

And, though nice of you dropping that tear,
  There are some who may think it my due—
Did it never occur to you, dear,
  That the flower may have wearied of you ?

IN A BAY-WINDOW.

CHARLES HENRY WEBB.

All, yes, there's a change in the weather ;
    It does look a little like snow—
Though in this recess it seems summer.
    And around us these red roses blow.

There is scarcely a theme we've not touched on
    Secluded, but talking at large
From the latest lyric of Locker
    To the very last freak of Lafarge.

And now it has come to the weather—
    As you say, there's a feeling of snow :
But do you not think it was warmer
    In this window one winter ago ?

Whose landscape, that one near the curtain ?
    It is good ? I really don't know :
I am thinking instead of the picture
    Seen then where these Jacqueminots blow

Just the same sweet profusion of roses,
    A lady, a silken divan,
A vase—was it Wedgewood or Minton ?—
    And a gentleman holding a fan.

Was the talk then of art and the weather ?
    Who could say ? for their voices were low ;
But none then who saw them together
    Thought it looked in the slightest like snow.

Must I look at that thing on the easel ?—
    Naughty nymph, and a bad Bouguereau !
But you plainly prefer any picture
    To the one whose each detail you know.

You think it unwise to recall things ?
    Unwise !   It is wrong, on my life !
The weather's so different this winter—
    You are married—and I—have a wife.

Around us the same crimson curtains,
    Just as warmly the Jacqueminots glow :
But I feel the same chill that you speak of —
    In the air there is certainly snow !

THE DUET.

ELLA WHEELER WILCOX.

I WAS smoking a cigarette :
Maud, my wife, and the tenor McKey
Were singing together a blithe duet,
And days it were better I should forget
    Came suddenly back to me :
Days when life seemed a gay masque ball,
And to love and be loved was the sum of it all.

As they sang together, the whole scene fled,—
    The room's rich hangings, the sweet home air,
Stately Maud, with her proud blonde head,
And I seemed to see in her place instead
    A wealth of blue black hair,
And a face, ah! your face,—yours, Lisette,
A face it were wiser I should forget.

We were back — well, no matter when or where ;
    But you remember, I know, Lisette —
I saw you, dainty and débonnaire,
With the very same look that you used to wear
    In the days I should forget :
And your lips, as red as the vintage we quaffed,
Were pearl-edged bumpers of wine when you laughed.

222

Two small slippers with big rosettes
    Peeped out under your kilt skirt there,
While we sat smoking our cigarettes,
(Oh, I shall be dust when my heart forgets!)
    And singing the self-same air;
And between the verses for interlude,
I kissed your throat, and your shoulders nude.

     .   *   '   .   *   -

You were so full of a subtle fire,
    You were so warm and so sweet, Lisette;
You were everything men admire,
And there were no fetters to make us tire,
    For you were — a pretty grisette;
But you loved, as only such natures can,
With a love that makes heaven or hell for a man.

    *   *   *   -   *   *

They have ceased singing that old duet,
    Stately Maud and the tenor McKey.
" You are burning your coat with your cigarette,
And *qu'avez vous*, dearest, your lids are wet,"
    Maud says, as she leans o'er me;
And I smile, and lie to her, husbandwise,
"Oh, it is nothing but smoke in my eyes."

ILLOGICAL

SHE stood beside me when I gave
    an order for a bonnet.
She shuddered when I said, " And put
    a bright bird's wing upon it."

A member of the Audubon
    Society was she ;
And cutting were her comments made
    on worldly folks like me.

She spoke about the helpless birds
    we wickedly were harming :
She quoted the statistics, and
    they really *were* alarming.

She said God meant his little birds
    to sing in trees and skies :
And there was pathos in her voice,
    and tears were in her eyes.

" Oh, surely in this beauteous world
     you can find lovely things
Enough to trim your hats," she said,
     "without the dear birds' wings."

I sat beside her that same day,
     in her own house at dinner—
Angelic being that she was
     to entertain a sinner.

Her well-appointed table groaned
     beneath the ample spread.
Course followed appetizing course,
     and hunger sated fled ;

But still my charming hostess urged,
     " Do have a *reed bird*, dear,
They are so delicate and sweet
     at this time of the year."

HER BONNET.

MARY E. WILKINS.

WHEN meeting-bells began to toll,
  And pious folk began to pass,
She deftly tied her bonnet on,
The little, sober meeting lass,
All in her neat, white-curtained room, before her tiny
  looking-glass.

So nicely, round her lady-checks,
So smoothed her bands of glossy hair,
And innocently wondered if
Her bonnet did not make her fair —
Then sternly chid her foolish heart for harboring such
  fancies there.

So square she tied the satin strings,
And set the bows beneath her chin ;
Then smiled to see how sweet she looked ;
Then thought her vanity a sin,
And she must put such thoughts away before the sermon
  should begin.

But, sitting 'neath the preachèd Word,
Demurely in her father's pew,
She thought about her bonnet still,—
Yes, all the parson's sermon through,—
About its pretty bows and buds which better than
    the text she knew.

Yet sitting there with peaceful face,
The reflex of her simple soul,
She looked to be a very saint —
And maybe was one, on the whole —
Only that her pretty bonnet kept away the aureole.

FINIS.

13